# The Pastoral

Jon Lawrence

Copyright © 2014 Jon Lawrence

All rights reserved.

ISBN:1492955876
ISBN-13: 9781492955870

This collection was first published in 2014 by Create Space for Little Eden Books
First edition 2014.
© 2014 Jon Lawrence / Little Eden Books

Cover designed by Whippet Design
Little Eden Books
Keepers Cottage
Low Road
Walpole Cross Keys
King's Lynn
Norfolk
PE34 4HA

The right of Jon Lawrence to be identified as the author of this work has been asserted by him in accordance with the Copyright, Designs and Patents Act 1988

All rights reserved. No part of this publication may be reproduced, stored or introduced into a retrieval system, or transmitted, in any form, or by any means (electronic, mechanical, photocopying recording or otherwise) without prior written permission of the publisher. Any person who does any unauthorised act in relation to this publication may be liable to criminal prosecution and civil claims for damages.

www.littleedenbooks.moonfruit.com
www.jonlawrencewriting.moonfruit.org

The Pastoral

# DEDICATION

This book is respectfully dedicated to the memory of those who died during the First World War. Many of their true stories have been told in the context of this semi-fictional account.

George Butterworth

Ralph Vaughan Williams

# CONTENTS

| | |
|---|---|
| Acknowledgments | i |
| Chapter One | Pg 1 |
| Chapter Two | Pg 15 |
| Chapter Three | Pg 24 |
| Chapter Four | Pg 37 |
| Chapter Five | Pg 48 |
| Chapter Six | Pg 61 |
| Chapter Seven | Pg 71 |
| Chapter Eight | Pg 88 |
| Chapter Nine | Pg 100 |
| Chapter Ten | Pg 116 |
| Chapter Eleven | Pg 128 |
| Chapter Twelve | Pg 140 |
| Chapter Thirteen | Pg 153 |
| Chapter Fourteen | Pg 161 |
| Chapter Fifteen | Pg 171 |
| Chapter Sixteen | Pg 185 |
| Chapter Seventeen | Pg 197 |
| Chapter Eighteen | Pg 208 |

The Pastoral

Author's Notes      Pg 216

# ACKNOWLEDGMENTS

Thanks to the following people for their support and insight during the writing of this book:

Ralph Vaughan Williams, George Butterworth, Gerald Finzi, Barrington Pheloung, Thomas Newman, The RVW Society, Sandy and Claire Mears, Rich Hill, Ben Willis and Julie Lawrence.

Special thanks to my family – Kerry-Ann, Hayden & Austin.

# CHAPTER ONE

August 26th 1958

The soft early-morning light crept through the window of the study and steadily filled the room with a comforting heat, unlike the previous day, which was sticky, muggy and oppressive. The thunderstorm and deluge of warm rain which fell during the night had brought welcome relief to number ten Hanover Terrace. The house near London's Regent's Park was a majestic building. In cream-white paint and, at either end, as well as in the centre of the terrace, tall pillars of faux-antiquity rose like great stone deities. This twentieth-century acropolis had been home to Ralph Vaughan Williams and Ursula Wood since their marriage in 1953. As the shafts of morning light beamed through the window they illuminated tiny particles of dust, floating lighter than air over the desk and the large grand piano in the corner. The lid of the piano was closed and the instrument substituted as a table, a candelabrum on one side, a mug of coffee on the other and a host of papers and musical paraphernalia strewn randomly in between. The bookshelf by the door was piled high with musical volumes, scores and shellac discs, which protruded out from the shelves, while other levels were home to a baton, a hearing aid, a viola bow and a picture of the porcelain features of Adeline Fisher – his first wife. The wood throughout the room was finest mahogany, except for the perfectly polished oak floor on which a large Persian rug rested. The full-length velvet curtains added to the rooms opulence, as did the magnificent dark red leather sofa and high-backed armchair.

Ralph had risen early that morning in order to see the sunrise from the balcony outside his study. It was a simple pleasure but one that he had enjoyed since he was a child in Dorking, Surrey. He would climb to the top of the tall stone tower at Leith Hill and look out over the county as the sun crept above the horizon and into the morning sky. He thought he could see the whole world. Decades later, as he looked down the long bright terrace and into the sunrise he felt, that morning, that it was an especially beautiful event. He had no particular reason to feel so poignant, but nevertheless he felt his heart rise. He returned to the study to sit at the piano and work on a new piece that he had circling around in his head. The necessity to work fast was twofold. Firstly, a good idea, be it a melody, a harmony or a rhythm, doesn't stick around for very long. One must submit it to manuscript paper as quickly as possible before it escapes into the ether, never to return. Secondly, time is less a friend and more a foe at the age of 85, so despite slowing movements and wits, one must work quickly to develop and preserve the ideas for posterity. He worked at the piano for an hour or so until the fatigue in his eyes and mind convinced him to get up and pace about the room, and anyway the ideas had dried up, and not for the first time. He was reminded of this as he picked up a pile of papers from the top of his piano so that he could arrange them into some semblance of order. As he did so a small sepia picture slipped and fell to the floor. He bent down gingerly to pick it up, his downward-stretched hand shaking and he was instantly reminded of a time when he had no ideas at all. Not even a hint of a spark that might ignite the flame of creativity. The time was 1914 and the picture was of his dear friend and fellow composer George Butterworth. Ralph put the papers down on the stool by his piano, took the photograph and sat down at his desk. He ran his fingers along the frayed edges of the photograph and then over the diagonal crease in the top-right corner. He looked into the eyes of his dear friend and smiled softly. He began to reminisce. As he did so, Ursula entered the study carrying a tray of morning tea and toast. Ralph hardly stirred as she set the tray down on the piano. His wife, some 40 years Ralph's junior, a slim elegant woman with flowing dark brown curls, held in place by a hair-band on top of her head, poured the tea into a china cup.

'You're up early, darling,' she chirped. Ralph, still fixed on the photograph, in his partial deafness, did not respond. His attention was in another world, in another time. 'Ralph!'

He returned to the fifties with a flutter of his heart.

'I'm sorry, dear.' He looked up at her.

'Everything okay?'

'Yes, I'm fine. I hope I didn't wake you.'

She smiled, 'No, I have been awake for a while. I was sat in bed working on a poem.' She huffed, 'Not a very good poem, but there we go. Have you got everything ready for the recording tomorrow? Did you make any changes to the score?'

'No, I think it's fine.' He ran his fingers through his thinning grey hair. 'It's too late to change it now anyway.'

'It's never too late.'

'No. It is done. Anyway, I find that there comes a point where one must simply abandon a creation.' He dusted down the lapels of his tweed jacket, 'One can simply go on refining and refining, editing and editing until the cows come home. It doesn't always make it better. In fact the more time one spends on a creation the more time and opportunity he has to lose sight of the very things that inspired him in the first place. Anyway the orchestra is all rehearsed. I don't think they'd take too kindly to last minute changes. No, it *is* finished.'

'What next then?' She handed him his tea.

'What do you mean?'

'Well, do you think you have another symphony in you?'

'I don't know. Nine isn't a bad total. Beethoven only wrote nine.'

'Haydn wrote over a hundred.'

He smiled, 'Yes, well he was Haydn.' He took a shaky slurp of his tea. 'And they were only tiddly little things! I don't know what next. I have some Ealing producers who want me to write some more film music, but I'm not sure what I have left. These last few years I have written so much, but I never take it for granted that music will be in my head when I wake up. I feel tired.'

'Well you've been very busy lately,' she replied, 'it's bound to take a toll on you at your age.'

'No, I mean…' he paused, took a deep breath and looked meaningfully into his wife's eyes, '…*Tired.*'

Ursula understood what Ralph was trying to say, but talk of death was not something she wanted to get into, especially as she felt its truth and reality ever more acutely with each day with him. Instead she went over to the window, unlocked it and opened it to allow a gentle breeze to enter and ruffle the papers on the desk. 'Oh, rubbish! You're as fit as a fiddle. Now, come on! I want a piano concerto by lunchtime, and I will be in to check on you!'

After Ursula had left the room, Ralph's attention turned once more to the picture of George Butterworth. He turned it over and on the reverse side it read; *To my dearest friend Ralph. Hope is all we have. Your friend, George. 1914.* The elegant writing now faded, but the words were undiminished. He leaned forward, guided his ample body up and made his way to the piano and sat on the creaking stool. Ruffling through the papers he came upon a handwritten orchestral score, complete with deletions and amendments. As he looked at the score he heard in his head, the clear tones of a bugle playing a two-note motif. The interval of the two notes, a seventh rather than the more comfortable octave, echoed throughout his mind, as did the sound of machine-gun fire, deafening explosions and the cries of men meeting their maker. He shuddered and shook his head as if trying to shake off these memories. This exact sound had haunted him regularly for the last forty years. The musical hallucinations would often creep into his consciousness when he least expected. Each time they arrived he would fall into a painful reverie and could only escape it by the inquisitive touch of someone's hand.

He stood up again and made his way to the bookcase and filed through his records until he found something he had not seen for years, an early pressing of a recording of his Third Symphony- 'The Pastoral'. He picked it out carefully, so as not to scratch the shiny black surface, and carried it over to the 1920's gramophone which stood on its own little table by the window. He placed it gently on the rubber disc beneath and slowly began to wind the handle. As he turned, he heard the rattling of the mechanisms inside which reminded him of the distant rattle of machine-gun fire. The turntable began to spin and with trembling hands he clumsily set the needle down into the opening grooves. He sat back down in his chair at his desk as the opening crackles and hisses of the record began to sound. As the soft opening tones of the flutes emerged from the great horn that flowered out of the gramophone, he sat back and closed his eyes, and as he did so he heard the sound of the sea.

## August 4th 1914

The sea at Old Hunstanton was calm. The August bank

holiday sun stifled all beneath it. Ralph and George waded ankle-deep in The Wash. Their trousers, held up by braces, were rolled up to their knees and they carried their shoes in their hands. Their baggy white shirts ruffled in the warm breeze. Ten years earlier the two of them had been in the same area of Norfolk collecting folk songs. Now, as they splashed around in the shallows, they sang those very same songs together. This was a time of true contentment. Children played with their parents, both shaded from the sun by handkerchiefs tied in knots at the corners. They dug deep holes in the wet sand, as others played cricket nearby. The beach was rich with activity. Ralph wrote five long lines in the sand to create a stave and wrote a little melody. As he did so he sang the tune to himself.

'Very quaint,' remarked George. 'What is it?'

'Oh, it's just something I've had in my head for a while.'

'Let me have a go.'

'Be my guest,' Ralph replied.

George hovered above the melody for a moment, looking at it and considering its potential. Beneath the lead line he added another pattern, a counterpoint which weaved beautifully through the initial tune. Ralph stood watching with quiet admiration. They stood up above the piece, looked at each other, smiled and began to sing the music. Neither was the finest of singers and their efforts made them laugh uncontrollably.

'It's a nice counterpoint. Shame it'll be gone in the morning,' said Ralph.

'Bah!' dismissed George. 'If I didn't write it someone else would.'

'I wish I had your confidence. At my age I can't afford to see ideas washed away.'

As the early evening sun began to set the two made their way up the beach, followed by the incoming tide. They sat down for a moment in the sand dunes beyond large tufts of tall grass and discussed, as ever, music.

'So, what's next for you?' asked George.

'I've got a few performances coming up; The Sea Symphony next month and Thomas Tallis.'

'London?'

'Leeds.'

George picked up a handful of sand and let it sift gently through his fingers. 'What are you working on at the moment?'

'Oh,' said Ralph evasively, 'just a few bits and bobs.'

'Oh, come on. The greatest composer in England? Bits and bobs?'

'I'm not the greatest.'

'Well, you might be the most modest.' Ralph looked away uneasily. He was not comfortable with praise, especially from his closest friends. They, he concluded, were most likely to lie politely to him about his music. Undeterred, George pushed for more information.

'Come on, talk to me Ralph.'

'Well, in truth, I have very little. I have done a bit on the opera.'

'The opera?'

'Hugh the Drover.'

George snapped his fingers in realisation. 'Of course! Are you still working on that?'

'*Grinding* through it really,' sighed Ralph.

'Tough work?'

'I'm not sure I'm cut out for opera.'

'Yes, well you said that about your first symphony, and that worked out okay didn't it? I mean it was very successful.'

'Well, I suppose so,' replied Ralph. 'Anyway, enough about me, what are you up to?'

'I've been working on some sketches for a symphony.'

'Wonderful!'

'Well, it's just a collection of scribblings and doodles at the moment, but I feel good about it. It's really English but it's going to be really new. Not just the rolling hills of the

Downs or the white cliffs of Dover, but something that captures the real England – warts and all.'

The two talked for hours about everything to do with music, laughing heartily through their fond recollections of the previous trips to Norfolk gathering folk songs for the first edition of the *English Hymnal*, which Ralph edited. As they reminisced, back on the beach the evening tide came in and washed away the music from the sand, the profound symbolism of which would never be lost on Ralph.

Later that evening Ralph was last to the dinner table. The Strange Arms Hotel was a large brown stone-brick house which catered for the affluent very nicely. Many of its ample-sized rooms overlooked the beach and The Wash beyond. Waiting at the table was his friend and fellow composer Gustav Holst, thin, with long unruly greying hair and round, steel-rimmed glasses. Next to him was the wide-eyed George, already merrily intoxicated with sherry. The conversation was already at fever pitch and Ralph was barely noticed as he took his seat.

'What's going on?' he asked.

Gustav looked up from his argument, 'Haven't you heard?'

'Heard what?'

'About the war,' said George.

'What war?'

George rolled his eyes, 'The war with Germany. Asquith gave Germany an ultimatum. Get out of Belgium or face war.' He slurred his speech slightly, 'Well they're still there, so we're at war.'

'It has been coming,' added Gustav.

'Well yes, I know it's been coming... I just didn't think it would actually... come.' Ralph paused while his two friends offered him a moment to take in the enormity of the news.

'Are you alright, Ralph?'

A moment passed, 'Um, yes,' he said, far from being alright. 'Yes, thank you, Gustav.'

'Bloody Germans,' burped George. 'Who do the think they are?'

'They *think* they're a world power,' answered Gustav.
George rolled his unfocused eyes, 'The British Empire! That's what you call power. A real power. The king and God will be on our side.'

Ralph felt uneasy. 'I don't think it will be as simple as all that. Being powerful doesn't make you invincible. It just means you are there to be challenged, there to be knocked off your pedestal. Well, now we have been challenged and blind faith, misguided youth and jingoism won't be enough I fear.'

'Patriotism!' George replied.

'And you think you can bring down the might of German militarism by waving the Union Jack and singing the Lords Prayer?'

'What's the matter with you?' said George incredulously. 'You daft old fool.' He turned to Gustav, who by now was starting to feel rather awkward. 'What do you think? Surely the Kaiser is no match for the British Empire. We have a quarter of the globe to call on.'

'Forgive me, George. I'm a daft old spiritualist. Mysticism and all that lovely hogwash. I must agree with Ralph.' George rolled his eyes again, sat back in his chair and sulked. 'When I wrote The Planets, and when I was writing the music for Mars – The Bringer of War, I couldn't help feeling that there was something prophetic about it. The music seemed to suggest something… relentless. Something that couldn't be stopped. It was cataclysmic.'

'What is this?' mumbled George beneath his breath. 'Don't either of you two have an ounce of faith?'

Ralph replied, 'Faith in what?'

'Faith in Asquith, faith in England, faith in… in the human spirit.'

'It is the human spirit which initiates war.'

'Oh, Ralph for goodness sake!'

Gustav interjected, 'George, all we are saying is that one should exercise a little caution.' The drunkard huffed. 'We're not traitors. No one is committing treason here, but the Germans have a vast army. Thousands.'

'That's why they're asking for volunteers. We need to swell the ranks.'

Ralph looked in horror at George. 'Please tell me you're not thinking of enlisting.'

'Why not?'

'Because you'll get killed, you stupid boy!' shouted Ralph.

George looked at Ralph, his sherry eyes still struggling to focus, and rose unsteadily to his feet. He needed both hands to retain his balance. He smiled at both of them. 'Oh ye of little faith! I'm going back to my room.'

The next morning at the breakfast table Ralph was feasting on an excellent full English breakfast at the Strange Arms when George walked in and sat gingerly at the table. The two acknowledged each other politely but there was distinct air of unease. They had been friends for many years yet this was the first time they had had an argument in which both parties were unalterably opposed to the other's view point. They both loved the English folk song tradition, they both loved walking in the countryside, they even shared the same taste in wine, but on this crucial matter there was no budging from either side.

'I'm sorry,' said George. 'I behaved beastly last night.'

'No, I'm sorry.' Ralph waved his hands dismissively, 'My tone was hardly gentlemanly, or subtle for that matter.'

A moment of restrained English emotion passed. 'So,' said George trying to fill the awkward silence, 'when will you go home?'

'I shall catch the train later this afternoon.'

'I see.'

'And you?'

'I shall be off later as well but,' George added uneasily,

'I will be going via the recruitment office.'

Ralph sighed but tried not to let his feelings get the better of him. He put his hands in his pockets, and stared at his plate – to catch George's eye at that moment would have evoked a host of unwelcome emotions, and that was not the English way.

'So, last night was clearly more than drunken bravado.'

'Certainly more than blind jingoism,' said George with an ironic smile. His friend returned the smile, albeit sheepishly.

'Oh, my dear George, I do so worry about you.'

'I know. But I'm not stupid.'

'I never said you were.' George only needed to look his friend in the eye to remind him of last night's comments. 'Well… I didn't mean it. But this won't be like any other war.'

'How do you know?'

Ralph gathered his thoughts, 'Because we have come so far in the last fifty years or so. We've learned how to use electricity, we've learned how to make music come out of a little box in the corner, we've even learned how to send messages through the air to people hundreds of miles away. We are the most intelligent creature on the planet. We can use our insight for the good of mankind,' he paused, 'but think of the unimaginable terror we could now unleash, if we put all that we have learned into war.'

'I understand that, Ralph.'

'Do you really?'

'Yes. But I have to have faith.'

Ralph huffed caustically. 'Faith? Your god is no different to us. We are, apparently, made in his own image. Yes, he created the sun, yes, he created the moon and all the lovely flowers, but he also created cholera and typhoid.'

'One does not simply confine their faith to God.' He took a while to calm himself. 'I have to have faith in my country. I have to have faith that the people of England are… good.'

'And you feel we should sacrifice lives, maybe even *your* life, to show that we are… good?'

'If we don't do something *thousands* of lives could be sacrificed. I wish I could explain it. All I know is that it's the right thing to do. I just wish you would have a little more faith in me.' George rubbed his finger down his bushy, black moustache and headed over to the breakfast bar, then turned back to his friend.

'Where do you put your faith, Ralph?' He smiled and proceeded to collect his food, leaving Ralph standing uneasily in the diner.

With the hour or so that Ralph had spare before his ride to the train station, he decided to have one last visit to the beach. The joy and laughter of the bank holiday children had been replaced by a solitary old man walking his whippets along the shoreline. He watched them sprinting along the sands playfully while the old man tried to retain some semblance of control by whistling to them occasionally. He was, at least, pleased that George had promised to postpone enlisting so that they could wave him off at the train station. Ralph walked up to the waters edge and wondered how the war might affect him. At forty-one he was too old to fight even though, as a pacifist, he would have resisted a combat role. He thought about how it might affect his music and then immediately chastised himself for even considering it at all, especially at a time when others would lose their lives. On the other hand he was well aware of the power of music, the way it could lift spirits and unify people. He was also aware that, to many, he represented the music of England. His music *was* England. Perhaps it was his responsibility to galvanise the spirit of England through his music. As the waves came in and out he noted the uncertainty of the waters, today much more choppy and turbulent than yesterday and thought of the uncertain fate of his dear friend, George. Then, as artists do, he began to see the situation differently, from another angle. This time he noted the certainty of the sea. Live or die, lose or win, whether or not mankind destroys itself in a war to end all wars, the tide will come and the tide will go. Ralph meditated on this philosophy for a moment and it alleviated his concerns, but the thought of losing his young friend was enough to bring him back to square one.

Later that day Ralph and Gustav waved George away from the train station at King's Lynn. Ralph watched as his friend leaned out of the carriage window, shouting that he would promise to write. The poignancy and profundity of the sight of his dearest friend heading off down the train track into the horizon was not lost on Ralph. He feared for his friend yet he was also bursting with pride. As the billowing smoke from train faded into the distance, the heavens opened and a deluge of warm summer rain fell down on the two remaining men. They scrambled into the train station café and sat by the window watching the platform flood steadily. Initially they had nothing to say, or rather nothing that they *could* say. Ralph looked at his hands and stirred his tea continuously, while the slender Gustav doodled in his notebook. Finally, after a large waitress had brought them both a piece of lemon cake and thumped it down on the table, Gustav broke the silence.

'He'll be okay, you know.'

'I wish I shared your confidence.'

'Yes, well it's his choice.' Gustav took his spectacles off and cleaned then diligently with his handkerchief.

'But it's the *wrong* choice.'

'That depends on where you stand.'

'What do you mean?' asked Ralph.

'Look, Germany has invaded France and Belgium. Who is to say they'll stop there? Who is to say that we won't be next on their list? And what do you say then? Will you be asking where all the George Butterworths are as the Kaiser storms into Whitehall?'

'I think it rather improbable?'

'But how do you know? You said it yourself, this will be a war like no other.'

Ralph bowed his head paused for a moment and thought of a response, but the truth of Gustav's words were undeniable. Placing his now clean specks back on, Gustav continued.

'You see, George is a doer. He wants to *do* something. He doesn't want to sit by and watch from the north shore. I fear the country will need thousands of George Butterworths if Germany is to be defeated.'

'I fear we will *lose* thousands of George Butterworths.'

'That's why we have to get behind them,' said Gustav. 'What's the alternative? Sit back and do nothing?'

'Well of course not, but…'

'But nothing Ralph!' Gustav's calm exterior and demeanor were momentarily breached. 'You can't have it both ways dear fellow. You can't have your rolling hills or the white cliffs of Dover, you can't have your larks ascending over pristine summer fields with great English folk tunes and all of that, without being prepared to fight for it.'

Gustav called the rather large lady over and asked for the bill before complimenting her on a splendid lemon cake. Then he picked up his umbrella and left, leaving Ralph to consider the truth, if indeed it was the truth, of his words.

## CHAPTER TWO

The train journey to the coastal town of Sherringham was too long for Ralph. It gave him too much time to think about the ramifications of direct action against the Kaiser and too long to consider the consequences of inaction. However, such thoughts were going through the head of almost everyone in Britain and Ralph realised that he would not be the only one with a personal concern, such as the participation of his dear friend George. In towns and villages, fathers would be talking to their sons about the war; some pleading with them to stay and others informing them of their duty to King and country – both terrified. Young fathers would be explaining to their own children why they would soon be going away for a while. The train eventually arrived in Sherringham and Ralph made his way home.

The evening was drawing to a close by the time Ralph arrived at his home, a flint-stone summerhouse surrounded by tall conifer hedgerows. Adeline was already in bed by the time he'd made his way through the front door. He ambled his way wearily up the stairs and saw his wife sat upright and reading next to her bedside lamp. She peered over the rim of her book and smiled at him. She seemed even more lovely than before he had left for Hunstanton. Her skin was smooth and delicate, like a little porcelain doll and her brown eyes were filled with such care and kindness. For that moment it was as though he was seeing her for the very first time. His heart rose, although he did not know why his feelings for her were so heightened at that particular time. Perhaps his fear of losing George had made him more acutely susceptible to the truth of mortality and the preciousness of the ones we care for.

'Good journey?'

'Long - very long.' He began to undress slowly, huffing and panting as he did so. 'How are you?'

She put her book down and placed it beneath her pillow. 'Aching!'

'Your knees again?'

'My knees, my ankles, me wrists. I keep telling myself that my mind is still working and that gives me some comfort!'

'Here, let me.' Ralph pulled back the bed-sheets and rolled Adeline's night gown up past her knees. He rubbed her knees with soft, gentle circling motions. Adeline sighed with relief. 'Any better?'

'Oooh yes!' she sighed.

'Shall I send for the doctor for you?'

'No, it's okay, love. You know what he said.'

'Perhaps he can give you something for the pain.' He felt helpless.

'I have something.' She leaned forward and kissed him softly on the lips.

He looked her in the eye and could not believe that through such pain, could be such beauty and elegance. He loved his wife with all that he had, unconditionally and unreservedly; he just wished that he could do something to alleviate the symptoms of agonising Rheumatoid Arthritis.

'You're so brave,' he said beaming with pride. He took

off the remainder of his clothes and got into his pyjamas. 'I suppose you've heard the news?'

'Who hasn't?'

He sat on the bed. 'There's more.'

'What?'

'George. He's going to enlist.'

'Oh!' said Adeline, not knowing what else to say?

'Yes, exactly, "Oh!"'

'Well, did you talk to him?'

'I tried, but he had made up his mind.'

There was a pause while Adeline digested the information. 'So, how do you feel about it?'

'How do you think I feel? I think he's mad. He doesn't know what he's doing. He seems to think that all he needs to do is read his bible, as if it is some kind of bloody instruction book.'

'I'm sure he has thought it through a little more than that, Ralph.'

'You think so?' he said doubtfully.

'Yes.' Adeline took hold of her husband's hands, 'He is an intelligent young man who knows what his path is.'

'He *thinks* he knows.'

Adeline paused for a second and drew breath realising that Ralph was just as set and stubborn in his contention as George, no doubt, was.

'You're not his father, Ralph.'

'I know.'

'Then stop acting like you are.'

'I'm not.'

Adeline smiled kindly at her husband, 'Yes you are. You always do. You always have.' The resigned look on Ralph's face suggested that he couldn't argue with his wife on this occasion. 'The way you look at him, the way you talk to him, even the way you describe him to friends is nothing short of… well, paternal pride.'

'I *am* proud of him.'

'And you should be, but you have to trust him a little

more.' Ralph looked forlorn. 'Now, come to bed. I've missed you.'

George stood in line at the village hall in Warfdale, Yorkshire which doubled as an army recruitment centre. The line itself was not particularly long, eight or nine men. George knew each one of them. Ten years earlier he had been at school with most of them playing soldiers in the playground, now they would prepare for the real thing. There was the stocky figure of Thomas Aldrigde, standing firm at the front of the queue. At last, thought George, someone has found a use for the school bully. Thomas had settled many an argument outside the school gates or, later, outside the pub with his bare hands and now he was going to be let loose with a rifle. Third in the line was Terry Halleton a thin child-like figure who was actually a year older than George but carried himself with an air of uncertainty and trepidation. George looked at him and feared that he would not last five minutes on the battlefield. Behind the apprehensive Terry stood two jovial characters, Arthur Jones and Eddie Widmark. Arthur, with his fresh, freckled face and ginger hair, and Eddie with his curly black locks and prepubescent-like stubble growing in patches beneath his nose, laughed uncontrollably. Their high spirits and confidence made George smile initially, but as he watched them he heard the cautionary words of Ralph and the corners of his mouth turned down somewhat.

Eventually George made it to the front of the queue. A tall, masculine soldier, in all of his military finery, medals and pistol, stood immaculately at the table while a recruitment clerk filled out the necessary paperwork. The soldier, who was in his late thirties, appeared strong and was ruggedly handsome. His air of authority intimidated George initially.

'Name?' he demanded.

'Butterworth, Sir. George Butterworth.' The clerk

entered the information.

'Age?'

'Twenty-nine, Sir.'

'Occupation?'

'Composer, Sir.'

'What?' asked the soldier incredulously.

'I'm a composer, Sir. I write music.'

'I know what a composer is.' The soldier stopped for a while and looked at George from head to toe. 'So, a composer.'

'Yes, Sir.'

'What do I want with a composer?'

George was uncertain, 'Well I…'

'Are you fit?'

'As a fiddle, Sir. No pun intended, sir.'

The soldier raised a smile. George stared straight ahead and stood firm and upright. The soldier then ambled his way around George as he stood stone-like. He noticed George's rather un-muscular frame.

'What do you do to stay fit, Butterworth?'

'I dance, Sir.'

'You dance.'

'Yes, Sir. I am also a professional morris dancer.'

'A morris dancer?' asked the soldier doing his best to contain a smile. 'Tell me Butterworth, why do you think you would make a good soldier?'

'Because I believe, Sir.'

The soldier was slightly taken aback by the readiness of George's response and the conviction with which he delivered it. He paused for a while.

'What do you believe, Butterworth?'

'I believe the German's need to be defeated, Sir; that the people of Belgium and France have the right to freedom, Sir.' He took a breath, 'And I believe that my God and my King will guide me through, and that evil will not prevail, Sir.'

The soldier looked at the recruitment clerk and shared

an approving smile. He turned back to George.

'A very nice speech Butterworth,'

'Thank you, Sir.'

'How long did you work on it?'

'All last night Sir. I'm more adept at writing music that writing speeches.'

'Clearly, Butterworth. You sounded like a ponce.' George smiled. 'Have you ever fired a pistol, Butterworth?'

'No, Sir.'

'A rifle?'

'No, Sir.

The soldier sighed, 'Have you ever *held* a gun?'

'No, Sir. I was rather hoping someone would show me.'

This time the soldier could not contain his smile or even a little laugh. He looked at his colleague once again, who also smiled.

'Well, Butterworth, you'll need to fill out a couple of forms, but I'm sure there is room for a morris-dancing composer in the army.'

George, still standing tall, raised a little smile of pride.

A week had passed since Ralph had waved is friend off from the train station, but George had never been far from his thoughts. Throughout the week Ralph had pottered around in the garden and had tried to read through a number of books, but could not focus his mind. He sat in the kitchen writing musical doodles on his manuscript paper but came up with nothing of any real note. Musical inspiration was usually close at hand for him, but for the first time in his life he was lost for ideas. He spent some time playing through some of the melodies that he and George had collected ten years earlier in the hope that he might ignite some kind of spark. Nothing.

On the first day in September Ralph received a letter which had been forwarded from his London address. He sat down in the garden in the late summer sun, among the eight-foot tall sunflowers that he was so proud of, and opened the letter. It was from George.

*My Dearest Ralph*

*I enclose a photograph with a little dedication to you, my dearest friend whom I have admired for so many years. I am aware of your objections to my involvement in the war effort, but I hope that it will not come between us as friends. I wish I could explain to you why I feel the need to do this but, alas, I fear I shall never be able to — we are both too strong in our convictions.*

*But my dear friend, please keep one word in you heart — for me, for you and for all of England. That word is HOPE. I hope to see you again and share music as we have done for so many years. I hope that this war will be swift. I hope that I shall survive it. Sometimes hope is all we have and is the only thing which sustains us through our trials. Keep your hopes for me, Ralph.*

*Your devoted friend*

*George.*

Ralph pulled out the accompanying photograph and admired the proud-looking George in his military uniform and read the dedication; *"For I know the plans I have for you, declares the Lord, plans for welfare and not for evil, to give you a future and a hope." Jeremiah 29:11.*

Ralph, an agnostic by inclination, was moved by the dedication. His eye flirted with a tear but in a very English manner he managed to control his emotions. Just then Adeline came into the garden with a cold glass of lemon cordial. As she placed the drink on the table next to him, Ralph put the letter and photograph in his pocket. Quite why he was doing this he was unsure. Something inside him was telling him that this was a profoundly private moment.

'What have you got there?' she asked.

'Oh, it's just a letter from the publicist.'

Without suspicion Adeline kissed him on the head and left him in the morning sun.

Ralph was a thinker. At every opportunity his mind would consider all sorts of things from philosophical subjects, religion, nature and his own existential place in the grand scheme of things. The problem with thinking too much is that it can quite easily lead to paranoia. As Adeline disappeared into the kitchen he wondered what people would make of his stance on the war. Now he was something of a public figure he was bound to be questioned on his ideological and moral position. The problem was that he had been so caught up in his concerns for George that he had hardly stopped to think about whether or not the war was justified. His speeches to George were primarily an emotive plea to him to try to dissuade him from active duty. He couldn't deny that in this case the Kaiser was the aggressor or that they should be driven out of Belgium and France. Yet all the bunting around the town halls and recruiting offices, all the national pride in the country's aim to liberate those who had been invaded and all of the hearty songs of the early soldiers in the streets preparing for battle, couldn't disguise a glaring hypocrisy for Ralph. For hundreds of years, he thought, the British have sent missionaries to every corner of the globe to change indigenous views of religion, inflicting Christianity on other faiths. The commonwealth now covered a quarter of the world and how much of the land, culture and wealth acquired were claimed peacefully or without any aggression on the part of the British? He recalled the Boer War, which had ended only twelve years earlier and was amazed that now England was taking the moral high ground when it was little more that a decade ago that the Britain had interned POWs in transit camps outside Cape Town, before sending them off to far off parts of the Empire. How moral or, indeed Christian was that.

Ralph got up and strolled around the garden, taking in the scents of the pink and white roses as he passed them. But his mind was still reeling. He decided that his thoughts should be private. If questioned he would offer his support for his fellow countryman but would decline to discuss his views on the war. He loved his country and he had spent the early years of his life as a composer proving so. He had managed to build a reputation as not only a fine composer but also as an artistic ambassador for all that was beautiful about Britain. To speak out now, however balanced or justified his argument, would be to undo all of his life's work and jeopardise his future career, and with Adeline's illness getting progressively worse, he needed to ensure that he could pay for her treatment.

As he watched the swifts and swallows playfully swooping through sky, gathering food on the wing to sustain their return trip to Africa, the beauty of the garden and, indeed, life seemed to be overwhelming. The skylarks in the fields beyond the stone garden walls seemed to be singing more sweetly than ever, their song carrying effortlessly on the wind. The roses, carnations and rhododendrons appeared more colourful than in his most vivid dreams. The smell of the lavender farms near by seemed more potent than ever. And yet, such beauty was tempered by the thought that an ugliness so unimaginable might soon destroy everything.

That night Vaughan sat at the piano in his study with pen and paper but still nothing was forthcoming. He tried once again to initiate an idea; he read – Whitman, Shakespeare and W. Somerset Maugham, he looked at his pictures of Adeline, but even her soft loveliness could not bring music to him. All the loveliness of the garden earlier that day had failed to penetrate his creative mind. So, he sat there in the darkness and with a strange numbness, watched the sun set through the windows of his study.

# CHAPTER THREE

A week or so later Ralph guided Adeline into the town. Sherringham was a hive of activity that morning. Bunting hung colourfully between street lamps and the trees. Kitchener's stone-cold face seemed to call to Ralph from every window and every door. Children ran joyfully in the street waving their little union jack flags. Choruses of 'It's a Long Way to Tipperary' were carried enthusiastically by the hearts and voices of men, women and children as they swarmed around the town hall. Union Jacks and St George's flags hung from the windows of the red-brick hall and the clock face, which stared out over the little town, seemed to stop for a brief while. The activity was due to a recruitment drive outside. Passing men and boys were beckoned in by recruiting officers from the navy and the army to sign up for active service with the promise of adventure and ultimately victory. Young men with young girlfriends or wives, eager to prove their manhood climbed the steps of the town hall to rapturous applause from the townsfolk. Each was received with joyful reverence and spontaneous rounds of 'For He's a Jolly Good Fellow.' Those who had only turned eighteen in recent weeks or months strutted with chests puffed out and smiles widening as they prepared to grant Kitchener his request.

Yet, at the back of the crowd, Ralph watched on in dismay. He wondered why they all couldn't see it. It seemed so obvious. He looked at their faces, smiling and laughing, and feared they would soon be crying and grieving. He feared that those standing on the steps of the town hall like heroes had not the first idea of the terror which would await them. As with every war throughout history the elders would sacrifice the younger generation and the youth would, seemingly without question, take up the challenge. Ralph turned away from the scene, leading Adeline by the arm.

'I can't watch this,' he said.

'Ralph?' she tried to pull him back. 'What's wrong?'

'They don't know what they're doing.'

'It's their choice.'

'That's just it; it's *not* their choice.' He took a handkerchief out of his waistcoat pocket and dabbed the first signs of perspiration from his forehead. He became agitated. 'It's Kitchener's choice. These... these... boys are simply obliging him.'

Adeline's face became stern, she sighed. 'What do you want Ralph? What do you want? Do you want us to send a train full of geriatrics out to France?'

'I want it all to stop!' he snapped.

'Soldiering is a young man's game. That's just the way things are.'

'Yes, and that is *exactly* what they think it is – a bloody game. Its cowboys and Indians. They're little toy soldiers, and like all toys they'll end up broken and forgotten. Who do you remember from the Boer?' Adeline was silent. 'My point exactly.'

'Look Ralph, whether it's a game or not. You can't change it. *You* can't change anything. It's got nothing to do with politics. If it wasn't Kitchener it would be someone else, someone else you wouldn't approve of. You think they've all been duped into fighting. Maybe some have, but give them some credit. They're not stupid. Beneath all that bravado, behind all the bunting and the hip-hip hoorays are men who are scared to death. Scared *of* death. Of course they're smiling, they are proud. They're just as proud of their country as you are, Ralph. But we can't all be national treasures, you know. The only difference between you and them is that they have no way of showing their pride, until now. And of course they are smiling, would you have them weeping their way to France? The war would be lost before it had barely started.' She took a step back from her onslaught and took a deep breath. 'It's primal. For thousands of years, if you believe Darwin, we have fought to protect our own, to protect our homes and to protect the things that matter to us. In the grand scheme of things we're but a step up from a monkey guarding his branch in a tree or protecting his troop.'

'Yes, but we're not protecting our branch. We're fighting hundreds of miles away in France and Belgium.'

'Yes, for now.' She took a few painful and unsteady paces away from Ralph and turned back to him. 'I can't make you see. You have your mind made up. It's just a shame; I thought you held the people of this country in higher esteem.'

Later that afternoon the weather took a turn for the worse. The rain poured down on the bunting and later, as the evening drew near, Ralph watched the hailstones bouncing six inches off the ground outside. He had been thinking about his wife's words and while there was truth in her words, he couldn't deny his own convictions. He sat in the kitchen and lit a couple of candles and began to write a letter to George.

*My Dear Friend George*

*Just a short note to thank you for your letter. I wish we had parted on more comfortable terms but I want you to know that I respect your decision to fight. I'm still not sure I completely understand it, but it is your decision. I am also sorry that my views on your faith may have been somewhat disrespectful. I am not a man of God, but I do consider myself a man of faith. We all put faith in different things. You believe in your God and Jesus, while I put my faith in family, and in this case, you. I have faith that you have made the decision that you feel is right for <u>you</u>. I only ask one thing of you – come back!*

*Your friend*

*Ralph*

He read the letter back to himself silently, but in his mind he heard George's voice so clearly that he almost wanted to talk back to him. He sealed the letter, left it on the table as the light faded and blew out the candle. He went into the study where Adeline was playing the cello for the first time in months.

'Bach!' he remarked.

'Yes, I thought I'd pick the old thing up again.'

'Sounds lovely.'

'Hmm,' she grimaced. 'I'm not sure. My hands are sore, I can't seem to grip it'

'Really, it was beautiful. Take it from me.' He smiled, 'I am a professional, you know.'

Adeline looked up from her cello and smiled back. 'I'm sorry.'

'Don't be silly.'

'No, I'm sorry. I shouldn't have said those things to you. It was beastly of me.'

Ralph stood behind her and tenderly placed his arms on her shoulder.

'No, I'm the one who should be apologising. You were right.' He squeezed her a little tighter, 'You're a woman, you always are.'

She smiled and took hold of his hand.

'You shamed me,' he said.

'I didn't mean to.'

'No, it's okay. I needed it.'

'Ralph,' she pulled his hand to her face. 'Don't, you are a good man.'

'I just didn't want to see it. In some ways I still don't want to see it. But closing my eyes isn't going to make it go away.'

'You just need a little…'

'Faith?' he interrupted.

'I was going to say, you just need a little… hug.'

Ralph laughed. He leaned forward and kissed her softly on the neck. She sighed happily. He kissed her again. Once again she exhaled in pleasure. Ralph kissed her again, this time allowing his lips and tongue to gently caress her neck and shoulders. She reached behind her and ran her fingers along the nape of his neck. Sensing her need for physicality and tactility he reached over and lightly touched her chest. She shivered and hundreds of tiny little lumps were raised up and down her arm. He reached further and placed his hand down the neckline of her dress, beneath her undergarment and took her breast, passing his finger over her nipple. In turn she pressed his hand on her body more firmly.

'I think it's time for bed, she whispered.

The barracks at Durham was bustling with activity. There was an excited buzz of conversations, peppered with exclamations and shouted orders from the superiors, desperately trying to gain some kind of order. The late and unexpected heat of the final days of September created a fusty smell, the scent of men sweating heavily. George, unaccustomed to the smell, heaved. He'd be glad when the winter came, he thought. George was issued his rifle and was instantly uncomfortable with its weight. He was also issued a bayonet which he fumbled with before finally fixing. Then Captain Houghton, a tall geeky man with a strange hooked nose, and smartly parted mousey hair, bellowed his instructions to the new recruits.

'Right, gentlemen, make your way to the rugby pitch on the double, please!'

George and the rest of the recruits headed noisily over to the park and were told to stand beneath the goal posts. The conversation carried on while Houghton waited for their attention. Soon he grew impatient for quiet and so took out his pistol and fired it no higher than two feet over the heads of the restless crowd. The group hit ground in unison, and silence was achieved instantly.

'Jesus Christ!' said Jenkins, a particularly mouthy man, just out of his teens.

Houghton with complete nonchalance subtly raised an eyebrow at the soldier. He beckoned him forward.

'Come here soldier.' Jenkins looked worried and hesitated. Houghton took his pistol and this time fired five yards in front of Jenkins. 'Please, if you would be so kind, soldier.'

Jenkins moved forward anxiously. 'Sir?'

'Do I look like I've got a fucking knighthood, soldier?'

'No, Sir.'

'No? Are you suggesting that I am not worthy of a knighthood?'

Jenkins was at a loss for the right words. Like a naughty schoolboy he lowered his voice and his head. 'Um, I don't know… um…'

'Captain! Captain Houghton.'

'I don't know Captain Houghton.'

'You felt the need to speak?'

'Yes Sir…' Houghton snarled before Jenkins quickly corrected himself. '…I mean Captain Houghton. I'm sorry. I was just a… a… l-l-little surprised.'

'Would you care to repeat those words for us,' Houghton asked patronisingly.

'No, Captain Houghton.'

'Please do.'

'I didn't mean to.' Jenkins became visibly frightened. 'I just meant…'

'Indulge me,' said his superior taking a step nearer to Jenkins face until they were almost nose to nose.

'Jesus Christ, Captain,' he muttered under his breath.

'I'm sorry soldier, I didn't hear you.'

Jenkins gulped, took a deep breath shut his eyes and repeated.

'Jesus Christ, Captain Houghton.'

'My dear fellow, that is blasphemous.'

'Yes, Captain Houghton. I am very sorry.'

'You're sorry?' The calmness of the captain's voice only served to terrify Jenkins further.

'Yes, Captain Houghton.'

'Hmm, what's your name soldier?'

'Arthur, Captain Houghton.'

'Surname, soldier! Your surname. I'm not your fucking friend, we're not on first-name terms here. What is your surname, soldier?'

'Jenkins, Captain Houghton.'

'I see Jenkins.' Suddenly Houghton put his left hand on the new recruit's shoulder and with his right delivered a powerful punch to the stomach which sent Jenkins crashing to the ground. The soldier was bent doubled, desperately trying to regain his breath. Before he had chance to breathe properly Houghton lifted him up by the collar of his coat and addressed the rest of the troops.

'Gentlemen,' he said without remorse or emotion, 'This is how we deal with blasphemy in the army. There will be no taking the Lord's name in vane. Where you are headed you will *all* need the lord, so I suggest you stay on his good side.'

Jenkins struggled to his feet, still trying to catch his breath. As he did so Houghton delivered a blow to the back of his head with his forearm sending the boy to floor once again.

'Did I tell you to stand up, Jenkins?' he asked in a patronisingly polite tone. The soldier battled to his hand's and knees but the captain placed his boot on Jenkins' back and stomped him to the floor.

'Did I ask you to get up, *at all*, Jenkins?'

His face in the mud, Houghton put the toes of his other boot on Jenkins' fingers and pushed down hard as the soldier began to weep.

'No, Sir,' grizzled Jenkins

'Captain! For fuck's sake!' he pushed his boot down harder on Jenkins' fingers.

'Aaagh!' he exclaimed, 'No, Captain Houghton.'

'You see gentlemen, here in the army, there are rules. You are here to follow the rules. I will tell you to do something and you will do it. You will not disobey orders. If you do, the consequences will be severe. Now, let's see how you gentlemen can handle a bayonet. Get into pairs, please.'

Houghton relinquished his hold and walked away, leaving Jenkins weeping as loud as he dared in the mud.

Later that evening in the canteen George was eating with what seemed like hundreds of soldiers and he thought about the day's training he had endured. His hands were blistered from gripping his rifle so tightly. During the training Captain Houghton had shown the recruits how to pierce the belly of an enemy soldier. All he could hear in his head were the words, 'Forward, stab, Twist! Forward, stab, twist!' over and over again. The barrow sacks filled with hay and sand were easy enough to attack, but George contemplated that it would not be so straightforward in the heat of battle when a German soldier would be trying to do exactly the same thing to him. Still, his conviction was resolute and steadfast, although any romantic or idealistic premonitions were now truly gone. Houghton had seen to that. He had been shocked by Houghton's brutal and cruel nature but George reasoned that the army needed discipline in order to function and that those such as the cocky and garrulous Jenkins needed putting in their place. Until that afternoon George had never heard a gun fired.

As he took a sip of his milk he heard a man behind him whistling a familiar tune. At first it was a little fragmented but soon, within the distracting din of the canteen, he began to put all of the motifs together and realised that in was his own tune; *On the Banks of Green Willow*. He turned around and there behind him was the welcome face of fellow composer Geoffrey Toye and, behind him, yet another friend and composer, Reggie Morris.

'Geoffrey!' shouted George.

'Georgie!' replied a stunned Geoffrey who, in turn, nudged Reggie.

They greeted each other with firm handshakes and manly slaps to the shoulders.

'What on earth are you doing here Georgie?' asked Geoffrey.

'I'm planning to take up crochet! What d'you think I'm here for, you silly fool?'

'I didn't think this would be up your alley, old chap,' commented Reggie folding his stocky muscular arms.

'I can't imagine it's up anybody's alley,' interjected Geoffrey putting his hands in his trouser pocket.

'Well, quite!' Reggie replied. 'But who would have thought it? Three composers, all heading for the front.'

'I'm rather looking forward to a *mano et mano* battle with Mr. Schoenberg,' declared Geoffrey. 'Bloody smart arse!'

'You can't shoot somebody for being a better composer than you, my dear fellow,' replied George.

'Oh well, I have to make do with Strauss,' he chuckled, 'think of it as payment for that bloody 'Til Eulenspiegel!'

'I rather liked it,' replied Reggie.

'You can't now!' Geoffrey added facetiously. 'They are the sounds of the enemy.'

'You'll have to make do with the French, Geoffrey.'

'Oh good heavens no, I think I've had enough impressionism to last me a lifetime. I just want to hear a damn good tune that I can sing along to, rather than that hoity-toity, watery rubbish.' He ran his hand over his slick black hair. 'Anyway talking of watery old rubbish, how's Ralph.'

Reggie chastised his friend, 'Geoffrey!'

'Oh, I'm only pulling his leg, old boy. Mind you he did study in Paris for a while. Ravel, wasn't it?'

'Yes,' answered George. 'He's fine. I saw him a few weeks ago, although I don't think he approves of my fighting.'

'He's a pacifist, of course he doesn't,' Geoffrey replied indignantly.

They all sat down and rested their forearms on the tabletop. George sipped a little more of his milk.

'There's no need for talk like that, Geoffrey.'

'Well, I'm sorry George but the war isn't going to won by those sitting down on their backsides telling us that we shouldn't be fighting, like patronising headmasters. It'll be won on the battlefield by those who could be bothered to fight for their country – including the pacifists.'

'It's not a case not being bothered,' George protested, 'it's about finding a way to resolve a conflict without resorting to killing you or me.'

'We're past the time for words now though, Georgie,' added Reggie.

'I agree but I don't feel that attacking Ralph is in anybody's best interest, or, for that matter, particularly fair.'

Geoffrey could see that he had offended George and there was a moment of unease and silence which needed to be expelled. He was aware of his friendship to Ralph and knew how highly George regarded him.

'I'm sorry, dear fellow.' George backed off a little. Geoffrey continued, 'I just feel that in this war we will need to be together, united. We can't afford any half measures. Not now. Nobody ever ended up drawing a war; it's win or lose, live or die.'

George looked at Reggie who was nodding in agreement with Geoffrey. There was something undeniable in what Geoffrey had said and George, at that moment was lost for words.

Adeline was once again in the study playing her cello. Her frail fingers occasionally slipping off the strings. Physically, it was an ordeal for her. With every bow she felt searing pain shoot through her elbows and wrists. However, mentally, the music sustained her and calmed her mind and soul. As she played Ralph walked in, placed his hands in the pocket of his cardigan and watched from the doorway admiringly. After a moment he made his way to the piano and began to accompany her. The duet, a Bach cello sonata, soared and swept through the melody, with Ralph punctuating the music with turns, trills and arpeggios. They were brought together in carnal union through the music and for a moment were oblivious of time and unaware of war. The only thing that mattered was the moment. The music came to an end and they shared a smile.

'I love Bach,' said Ralph.

'I love you,' she replied.

'I love you too.' Ralph's tone lowered, as did his smile. 'But I have something I have to tell you.'

Adeline put the cello down and placed her hands in her lap. She sat bolt upright. 'That sounds ominous.'

'I'm going to France.'

'I don't understand.'

'I'm going to join the army,' he said, putting the lid of the piano down. 'I'm enlisting.'

'But I thought you said… But you're too old to fight.'

'I'm not going to fight.'

Adeline rubbed her fingers to relieve her pain. She shook her head. 'So what are you going to do?'

'I'll join the medics.'

'What do you know about medicine?'

'Nothing, but they'll train.'

'But I thought you said…'

Ralph interrupted, 'I know what I said, Adeline. All the things I've said, all the things you've said, all the things that George said – that's all I've heard in my head over the last few weeks.'

'Then why the sudden support for the war?'

'I'm not advocating the war. I don't support it. But I can't sit by and watch the likes of George get slaughtered. I can't do much for them, but if I am there for them… if I can help just one, then when it's all over at least I'll be able to say I did something… good. I know it doesn't make sense.'

'No, it makes sense. I understand, but I'm just a little surprised.'

There was a pregnant pause. Adeline didn't know whether to burst with pride and hug him or erupt with anger and hit him. She decided on the former, anything less would have been hypocritical. However, she now had a new insight into Ralph's concern for George's participation in the war.

'You'd think that my guilt might be relived,' he said.

'You've done nothing to be ashamed of, Ralph.'

'I should have supported George.'

'Look, don't do this to yourself. What's done is done. Why should you feel guilty now?'

'Because… because…' He hesitated. 'I *do* want to help them. I *do* want to do some good, but there's a little voice inside me telling me that I'm only doing it for the sake of my own conscience.'

'To hell with *why* you are doing it. What matters is that you *are* doing it.' She stood up, moved gingerly to the piano and placed her arms around him. 'I love you Ralph, but you aren't perfect, and you'll never be as good as you want to be. You set your sights so high. You expect so much of yourself.'

He kissed her hand as it draped across his shoulder, then caressed it tenderly.

'You should stay with your parents.'

'I'll be fine,' she replied.

'I know you will, but it would help put my mind at ease.'

'I don't need looking after.' Ralph raised his eyebrows at her, she knew she needed help. 'I just need you, so make sure you come back to me.'

'I'll come back. I promise.' He kissed her hand once more, 'I promise.'

## CHAPTER FOUR

Southampton hummed with conversation. Parents, lovers, brothers, sisters and friends, almost in harmony, seemed to be saying the same things to their loved ones before they boarded the huge ship which would take them to France. There were verses of 'take care', choruses of 'I love you,' stanzas of 'I'm so proud,' repeated lines of 'come back safe' and then tearful refrains of 'I love you' once again. And yet within the tears was an air of national pride. Standing in the crowd so still as to be conspicuous, Ralph watched all of the proud business around him and searched for George. There was no sign. There was almost no way of distinguishing him from anyone else in the army. Everywhere he looked there was a sea of green uniform. They all seemed so anonymous. Ralph knew that the army obviously had to display a kind of visual unity but he couldn't help feeling that the thousands of young soldiers preparing to board the ship were like ants, all there in the defence of their majestic superior – all expendable. Ralph managed to contain his emotions within all of the tears, the embraces and the promises to return, until in front of him he saw a young father on his knees before a child who could have been no more than four. Standing with them was the child's grandfather. The father, a handsome, clean-shaven face with defined features took off his hat and ran his fingers through his wavy blonde locks.

'Edward,' he said, 'my dear, dear boy.'

'Yes Daddy?'

'I have to go now. Do you understand why?'

'Yes, Daddy. There are some naughty men over the sea... and you are going to help tell them off.'

The father smiled. 'Yes, Edward.'

'Are they very naughty, Daddy?'

'Yes, I'm afraid so.'

'Are you going to give them the cane?'

The innocence of his child was too much to bear and as the tears welled up in his eyes, the father pulled his son as close as he could. 'Something like that, my boy,' he replied.

Ralph watched on as the father held Edward as hard as he could. It was as though he were trying to provide a lifetime of embraces in one perfect hold.

'You promise to be good for your Grandad?'

'Yes.'

'Say it then, boy.'

'I promise. I promise I'll be a good boy.'

'I love you son,' he ran his fingers through the little boy's hair. 'I love you so, so much. Ever since I first held you I have loved you so very much. And I am so very, *very* proud of you.'

As he rested his head on his son's tiny shoulder he wept. He pushed his face deep into his son's jacket and the placed his nose into his son's hair and breathed in deeply, as if trying inhale all of his son's love.

'I love you too Daddy,' said the child, completely unaware of the magnitude of this farewell. 'When will you be back?'

The young man looked up at his own father and briefly caught Ralph's eye too, which was now beginning to shed a tear. The man wiped his face, still and firm in his final embrace, before pulling away slowly.

'As soon as I can, boy,' he stood up and ruffled his son's hair before brushing away an imaginary piece of dust of his son's collar, a final act of paternal care. 'As soon as I can.'

Ralph watched as the man hugged his own stone-faced father one last time before walking off to board the ship. Ralph, for a moment thought about his own father, who had died when he was only a toddler. The faint outline of his father's face and echoes of his kind features briefly interrupted the din around him. Then the man disappeared beyond the gangway and into the ship's belly. The steadfast grandfather then caught Ralph's eye next to him. He moved up to Ralph stoically and stood right before him, face to face. He looked deep into Ralph's eyes as if looking for someone he knew, someone familiar, a friend, perhaps. Then, as if a light had been turned on, he flung himself at Ralph and hugged him tightly. He burst into a cataract of uncontrollable tears and repeated his son's name over and over. Ralph at first was at a loss as to what to do. In the end all he could do was hug the man back with all that he had. No words were exchanged. Ralph, looking over the shoulder of the grandfather who clung to him tightly, saw Edward standing perfectly still in the business of the crowd. He closed his eyes for a moment and as the brief darkness filled his world another picture emerged. He saw little Edward standing alone on the dock with the bodies of all the soldiers lying around him. Their corpses were bloody and mutilated. Carrion crows and seagulls picked at the soldiers and for a moment Ralph could hear their cries and the smell of decaying flesh came to his nose. Flies hovered over the scene while others crawled over the white faces of the dead. But most disturbing, Edward stamped and splashed in little puddles of blood as if playing in the street after a rainy day. He opened his eyes and blinked hard as if trying to expel the vision. Ralph also began to cry, but resolved to do so in as dignified a manner as he could. After a moment which seemed to last for ever the man pulled away from him and Ralph watched the tears run through the ageing cracks in his face. In silence they looked at each other for a moment before the grandfather took Edward by the hand and headed off through the crowd.

Once the soldiers had boarded and were waving to their families below, almost in unison they seemed to break out into spontaneous rounds of 'God Save the King'. Union Jacks fluttered everywhere. Hats were raised and waved in the air like grass in a summer meadow. Up on deck George wandered around aimlessly taking in the atmosphere completely unaware of his friend hidden within the crowd. The smoke billowed out of the huge steel chimneys on top of the ship and slowly, surely and worryingly it began to split the calm waters off Southampton dock and headed off into the English Channel. As the crowds began to disperse and the tumultuous din of crying mothers and fathers abated, Ralph was left standing, almost alone on the dockside. He wondered if he would ever see his friend again.

It took a few months for Ralph to arrange care for Adeline. Her parents were away travelling around Europe, making the most of the affluence they had worked hard for. By Christmas 1914 they had returned and Ralph and Adeline spent one more Christmas together. It was an intense time. They knew that within a week, Ralph would be off. Everything was concentrated. Embraces became tighter, kisses became more and more tender and each declaration of love became more honest and poignant. When they parted on the day before New Years Eve they tried to contain their emotions in as English a manner as they could, but tears were shed and hearts were broken. However, he was steadfast in his conviction; he would serve his country but in no way would he endorse the war.

It was a bitterly cold New Years Eve day in London. The whiteness in the sky was matched by the whiteness in Ralph's face, bar the red nose. The wind blew through the skeleton trees and seemed to offer ominous portents. Ralph stood outside the Duke of York Headquarters in Chelsea, took a deep breath and sighed before making his way up the steps and into the recruitment area.

He completed all the necessary paperwork and soon became at ease with the place. The army personnel were efficient but friendly. As he wandered around he noticed that most of the other recruits were, like himself, in their forties; men who were too old to fight but would offer their services to King and country in whatever way they could. Later on he sat on the steps outside HQ and wrapped himself in his new military coat to keep warm. He looked at a carbon copy of his admission form. No longer was he Ralph Vaughan Williams, the revered and famous composer; he was Private Vaughan Williams of The Royal Army Medical Corps Territorial Force.

'D'you mind if I join you mate?' a true cockney sound if ever it was heard.

Ralph turned round and standing behind him was a short stumpy man also in a new army-issued coat, only this one didn't seem to fit.

'Uhm, yes,' he replied, 'please do.'

'Bloody cold ain't it?'

'Yes it certainly is.' Ralph offered a friendly smile to the man.

'You nervous?'

'Yes.'

'Me too.' There was a moment of silence. 'My name's Harry. Harry Steggles.'

'Ralph,' they shook hands, 'Ralph Vaughan Williams.'

'Nice to meet you.'

Ralph was relieved that Harry didn't realise who he was, he felt rather uncomfortable with the attention which accompanied his notoriety.

'Likewise. What d'you do mate?

'I'm sorry?' asked Ralph, wondering how anybody could be this chirpy!

'What d'you do for a job? What's your line mate?'

'Oh, I'm a musician.'

'Bloody hell! Me too. What do you play?'

'Uhm, well I play piano and a bit of viola, if pushed.'

'You any good?' asked Harry cheekily.

'I do okay, enough to get by,' replied Ralph modestly. 'What do you play?'

'Me?' Ralph nodded. Harry pulled something out of his pocket. 'Harmonica. Look.'

Ralph took the harmonica from Harry and looked at it intently. It was beautifully ornate silver with a button for chromaticisms on the end.

'I've always been fascinated with these things. Such a lovely tone. I've always told myself that one day I am going to be the first person to write a harmonica concerto.' Harry smiled. 'An uncle of mine brought me one back from Germany many years ago, but I could never get on with it.'

'Oh, there's nothing too it. It's a simple case of inhaling…' he took in a deep breath, '…and exhaling,' then out.

'I say, could I possibly convince you to give me a demonstration.'

Harry smirked, 'Are you sure? Usually when I start to play me wife asks me to shut up.'

A little smile from Ralph. 'No, honestly, I should be most grateful.'

Harry licked his lips and then brought the instrument up to his mouth with an air of uncertainty. He hesitated for a moment and then began to play. Soon the sweet melody of Greensleeves filled the air around Ralph and as it did he was immediately transported back to the fields in Surrey where he grew up as a child. As the tune flittered through his brain he could smell the sweet honeysuckle in his childhood garden, he saw himself running in and out of the bright yellow rape fields near by. Then, he saw himself lying on his back in a summer meadow, the grass tickling the nape of his neck, only it wasn't grass, it was the feeling of the hairs on the back of his neck standing upright on account of the beauty coming from Harry's lips. Ralph was awakened from his daydream when Harry stopped playing.

Harry put the harmonica back in his pocket. 'Well, I never claimed to be an expert, but you get the gist of it.'

Ralph didn't quite know what words to choose. He hesitated for a moment and then, unblinking, the words chose him.

'It was perfection.'

As those words fell from his lips the moment was interrupted by a young voice, nervous and breaking with the early stages of adulthood.

'Mr. Vaughan Williams?' Ralph looked up. 'Please excuse me Sir, but you are Ralph Vaughan Williams, aren't you?'

Ralph felt uneasy. He looked at Harry. If he hadn't already told Harry his name he would have denied it. But now there was no escape from his fame.

'Uhm, yes it is… I suppose.'

'I'm most terribly sorry to trouble you Sir, but I am a great admirer of your music.'

'Oh, that's most kind of you.'

'Could I trouble you for an autograph? I have a copy of Whitman, I know you are a fan of his. I remember your first symphony, *The Sea*.'

'Yes, that's right,' he shuffled uncomfortably. 'Hum no… I should be delighted.'

'Thank you.'

'To whom should I write?'

'To me please,' the young man replied in awe.

'Um, no, I mean, what is your name?'

A little chuckle. 'Peter. Peter Aldridge, Sir.'

Ralph signed the Whitman volume. 'Which is your favourite?'

'Oh, The Wasps is a favourite of mine although I also enjoyed the London Symphony. I was at the premier at The Queen's Hall earlier this year.'

'Oh, I see,' feeling a little awkward. 'But I actually meant which is your favourite poem.'

Aldridge, clearly of good stock, blushed a little, 'Oh, I'm sorry. Er, I like um… *Adieu to a Soldier.*'

There was not a hint of irony in his response, but the innocence with which he delivered the line was not lost on Ralph or Harry. They looked at each other and, without uttering a word, erupted into uncontrollable laughter. Aldridge couldn't understand what all the light-hearted mayhem was about, but smiled sportingly. Ralph finished his dedication and Aldridge strolled away happily. Soon the hilarity subsided.

'I had no idea,' said Harry.

'What do you mean?'

'I had no idea that you were so important.'

'Yes, well I don't do blessings I'm sorry.'

Harry laughed. 'Oh, well. But seriously, I didn't know you were famous.'

'Well *you* didn't know me, so I can't be that eminent.'

'Yes but…' he seemed a little awkward.

Ralph was a little confused. 'But… what?'

'Well, I can't really imagine you in the pub with the dockers. You've done alright for yourself. Are you rich?'

'Does that matter?'

'Well no but…' Ralph raised his eyebrows. 'Well, put it this way, if the Germans hadn't started this whole thing, then we wouldn't be having this conversation.'

Ralph didn't want to get into a debate about class with Harry. He was aware of his fortunate affluence and often felt a sense of guilt. Instead he thought for a moment and gave a considered response.

'People are people. It's really not that difficult. Well,

not to me anyway.'

Harry smiled, completely at ease with his new friend.

The sky above northern France was dark. It was heavy and seemed to weigh down on the back of George, Geoffrey and Morris. The previous day had brought a deluge of freezing winter rain making the march between towns cumbersome and dismal. Private Butterworth of the Duke of Cornwall Light Infantry headed the group of recent soldiers without complaining. He listened to the complaints, and there were many, of those around him and at all times tried to provide encouragement or solace to his friends. Indeed he had already started to impress himself upon the opinions of Captain Houghton. Although Houghton, a disciplinarian of some repute, did not always agree with Butterworth's cheery demeanour – they were, after all, not there to enjoy themselves – he could not deny that George had built a rapport with many of the troops in the platoon and that he led by example.

George had come a long way both physically and metaphorically, since he first arrived in France. On his first day as he walked to the front with his new colleagues, he, along with the rest of the men, had started to sing. Soon there were loud choruses of *Rule Britannia* and *Jerusalem*. Then the hearty lyricism was interrupted as they passed two German corpses on the side of the road. The voices quickly trailed off into complete silence and all that could be heard was the sound of stomping boots and the breeze passing by. The corpses were ridged, like an eerie sculpture. The face of one soldier was completely missing, his head like a broken egg with jagged edges and darkly hollow inside. George had never seen a dead body before. Along with the rest of the group he stopped for a while, staring morbidly at the decaying body, buzzing with flies and crawling with various kinds of parasitic invertebrates. Soon the jingoistic melodies stopped once and for all. Although this was the shell of an enemy soldier George could not lose sight of the fact that wherever he was from, the deceased had a mother and father, perhaps a lover or even children. George had vowed to try to see all death in the same way. He surmised that the day he saw a dead body and recognised only a shell would be the day he would lose his humanity.

In his first three months George had killed two German soldiers. Quickly becoming adept with a rifle, he had sniped a pair of enemy low rankers who had dared to place their head above the recently dug trenches near the town of Ypres, and run toward the British trench. As he watched them fall everything around him had seemed to stop. The first soldier he had hit clean through the head and he was felled instantly, dead before he hit the ground. However, the second soldier was struck in the neck and although he was at least a hundred yards away George could see that the soldier had not died at once. He saw the soldier writhing on his back, holding his shattered throat. Even from that distance he could see the eruptions of blood shooting six inches above him. He heard cries from beneath the German trench line. 'Kasper!' they screamed, 'Kasper!' The soldier reached out his blood-soaked hand, pleading for rescue. Nobody came. George couldn't bear to see the man spluttering his last breaths away in such silent agony and so aimed again. This time, the soldiers head firmly in his sights, he shot and, to his horror, missed. He saw the dirt explode just to the left of the soldiers head. George could feel Kasper's fear running through his own veins, his heart pumped through his body so powerfully that his head began to bang painfully. The next shot was deadly accurate. A split second after the explosion from his rifle Kasper's skull opened up in a shower of crimson. George looked through his telescope and saw the static body of Kasper strewn on the ground with residual smoke from his bullet rising steadily in the air. That night he cried silently until the dawn broke. While the stars and moon were occasionally coloured from the red hues of flares overhead, he thought about Kasper. He wondered who he was, where he came from and even what dreams he may have had. He saw a mother in a country garden receiving a letter informing her of her son's death. In his mind he saw her slump to the floor; he heard her tears, her heartbreaking cries of, 'Kasper! Kasper!' Then her tone changed and her voice became the cries of his comrades, calling out to him as he lay bleeding in no-man's land. Knowing the soldier's name only made the killing more distressing for George. It personalised it. An un-named enemy, shot clean through the head, would be the legitimate killing of an anonymous soldier and, to many, could simply be seen as one of the ten green bottles falling off a wall. However knowing Kasper's name made George feel like a murderer. He tried to reason that Kasper would have had no hesitation in shooting *him* through the throat given half a chance but it was scant consolation.

After the incident George wrestled with other demons as well. He couldn't reconcile the religious contradictions. Back in Norfolk he had told Ralph that God would see England through, that God would guide him and keep him safe. Indeed, he had been kept safe, so far, but how much of that was to do with God? Did he, in truth, owe his safety thus far to luck, to the camaraderie of his platoon or to the inaccuracy of German fire? Where was God when he felled Kasper? Was He behind the sights of George's rifle, guiding it surely into the skull? Or, was He with the suffering German guiding him from one world to the next? Was this a God of strength or a God of compassion? Was it the same God who said, 'Thou shalt not kill?' Or, was it the God who sent a murderous wind into Rameses' city, murdering all of the first born? George would look up to the sky and pray earnestly for certainty but found only more contradictions.

# CHAPTER FIVE

It had just turned six in the morning. In a small terraced house in Bishop's Stortford, Mrs. Bloodworth poured two cups of hot tea and called to her guests.
'Boys!' she cried. 'Brew!'
Mrs Bloodworth, a kindly septuagenarian with curly silver locks and a faded white apron around her ample hips had grown fond of her guests. She had taken Ralph and Harry in when the authorities had asked for the general populace to help with the billeting of army personnel around the country. Following the mass recruitment to support the war effort it quickly became apparent that the army's accommodation simply wasn't substantial enough to house the thousands of extra troops and support staff that flooded into its ranks. Ralph and Harry made their way into the kitchen and sat at the table by the stove.
'Mrs. B you are a woman after my own heart,' said Harry.
'Oh, go on with you!' she smiled.
'I have been all around London and never found anyone who can make a brew like you.' He stood up and gave her a playful kiss on the cheek, Ralph chuckled.

'Steady on you. A kiss from a young man could do a mischief to the heart at my age.' She offered a plate of biscuits, Ralph politely refused so Harry gladly took an extra one. 'Anyway, I imagine you boys have another busy day lined up.'

'Oh, yes,' said Ralph.

'More marching I bet,' said Harry. 'Six miles yesterday.'

'Well, at least you'll be fit, my lad. We can't have you huffing and puffing and falling down in France.' She gave them both a motherly kiss on the head and left the room.

'This is driving me mad, you know,' said Ralph.

'What d'you mean? She's lovely!'

'No, I mean this training.'

'Oh, I see.'

'It's the routine, the monotony.'

'Oh, it's not that bad, surely?' said Harry, trying to inject a little light into the conversation.

'Up at five-thirty, walk six miles, lunch, squad drill, stretcher drill, first aid, lecture, back for tea; every day! And those bloody uniform inspections. We've been doing this for a year.'

'Well what did you expect, Ralph? It's the army. It's built on discipline and routine.'

Ralph rubbed his tired eyes and sighed. 'Yes, I suppose you're right. It's just that I'm really not used to such routine. One day I'm in London, the other I'm off to Leeds, the next day traveling to Edinburgh.'

'Yeah, well your rich aren't you?'

'What does that mean?'

'Nothing. But your money and position has removed boredom from your life. For the rest of us we live with routine all the time.'

'What position? I'm not the king, you know.'

'No, I know, but you mix with all that lot don't you.'

'What lot?'

'You know,' Harry said with a chuckle, 'all those big cheeses.'

Ralph didn't say anything. He was slightly irked by Harry's comments no matter how true they might have been. In particular he was annoyed by Harry's assumptions.

Harry continued. 'Take me, for example. I am a milkman. Everyday I go to the dairy at three in the morning, pick up my load, fill the cart and then I'm off on my rounds. I go to the same houses and see the same people everyday. It's great! I know all about the people who live there, what they're up to, how they're feeling… Then I come home, bring the money back, put it on the table, the wife puts it in her apron, she makes me a brew, I go to sleep for a while then I'm up for when the boy comes home from school. I wouldn't change a thing.'

'Well, it's not for me.' Harry shrugged his shoulders. Ralph continued. 'What I really want to know is when we will be off to France. What's the point in trying to resuscitate dummies stuffed with god-knows-what when we could be doing some good in France. We're just going over the same old rubbish, again and again and again.'

Ralph became more animated and was clearly not in a positive frame of mind. Sensing this, Harry took a moment to think. He took a sip of tea and wiped his lips dry with his forearm.

'You like folk music?' he asked.

'Folk music?'

'Yeah, folk music. Do you like it?'

'Well yes but…'

'Right tonight we're going out.'

'What? I don't underst…'

'Now drink up, Brass-Knob, we'll be late.'

Morris sat on the duckboards, his legs crossed, a pad in his lap and a pencil in hands, partially covered by fingerless gloves. He tapped the book and every-so-often a little idea would accost him. Sometimes he'd smile in quiet satisfaction, other times he would scrub out his musical doodle and sulk. Overhead shells would explode and the crackle of machine gun fire was ever-present. Geoffrey, appeared carrying his rifle wearily.

'Hello old boy,' said Morris. My word! You don't look quite the ticket. What's up?'

'I don't know. I thought I had a cold but I feel really rotten. I think it's flu.'

'Well you should get some rest,' said Morris. 'Here, take my coat.'

Morris took Geoffrey's rifle and propped it up against the sand bags which walled the trench and put his coat around his friend.

'Here, have some water.'

'Thanks.' Geoffrey took a swig from Morris's flask.

'How long have you felt like this?'

'A few days now.' He mopped his brow. 'I can't sleep. I haven't slept for days. Not properly.'

'Well, you can rest now.'

From up the line of the trench Captain Houghton came with his usual miserable expression. Morris stood to attention and saluted. Geoffrey took his time and wearily stood up and did the same.

'What's going on here gentlemen?'

'Nothing, Captain,' replied Morris.

'What's wrong with you, Toye?'

'Nothing, Captain.' He wobbled as he tried to stand firm. 'Just a little snivel I think.'

'Well, I think we can all overlook a little snivel, can't we?'

'Yes, Captain.'

'Good, because you are on sniper duty tonight, Toye.' The last few shades of pink and red seemed to drain away from Geoffrey's face until he was almost white apart from his lavender blue lips. Morris interrupted, 'Sir, I could take over for Private Toye tonight. If he's not feeling well I could…'

'He's got a cold Morris, for Christ's Sake,' Houghton interrupted. 'With men being blown to pieces all around us, I'm not going to make an exception for a fucking toff with headache.'

'But Sir…'

'Captain! I'm your fucking captain, Morris!'

'Sorry Captain. I meant to say…'

'I don't want you to say *anything* Private. I just want you to get out of the fucking way.' Morris was slow to move so Houghton stood almost nose to nose with him. 'Move!'

Morris stepped aside reluctantly and Houghton barged passed them both before turning back to Geoffrey.

'I want you ready for sniper duty in an hour, Toye.'

That night the stars were perfectly visible and the temperature plummeted. Morris and George huddled together on some sandbags beneath their coats desperately trying to keep warm. Geoffrey rested his fatigued head on his rifle looking out above the brim of the trench toward a dark horizon in the distance.

'I'm worried about Geoffrey,' said Morris.

'Yes, I know,' replied George, 'me too.'

'What should we do?'

'I'm not sure what we *can* do.'

'Houghton's asleep, we could take over. You and I could take turns. I'll do the first watch, you take over from me later.'

'No.'

'Why not?'

'Because if Houghton does wake up and sees you or I on Geoffrey's watch there'll be two privates up for a court marshall.'

Morris became annoyed, 'Well, then we'll have to pray that he doesn't wake up.'

'No, Reggie!'

'But look at him he can hardly keep his eyes open.'

'I know, but I'm not going to…'

There was a large rifle crack and Geoffrey was suddenly animated. In a blind panic with a child-like fear in his face he began to shoot indiscriminately into the distance. He shot wildly and then, with his freezing fingers, fumbled around for more bullets and then shot again, screaming as he did so. George and Morris ran to Geoffrey's side.

'What is it, Geoffrey?' George asked.

All the slumbering soldiers in the trench woke up and fumbled around for their weapons. Houghton stirred and rose to his feet. He picked up his rifle and ran to the scene.

'What's going on, Toye?'

Geoffrey didn't look away from his rifle and ignored the Captain. Houghton tried again but once more Toye was unresponsive. Houghton shouted to the men. 'Be alert men! Bosh attack! Bosh attack!'

George loaded his rifle and check the chamber of his Smith and Western revolver. Morris did the same before making the sign of a cross on his face and body and reciting the Lord's Prayer. Houghton picked up the periscope and looked out over the no-man's land. He ordered a flare which was duly fired into the air. As it ascended the night sky turned bright red, finally bringing some colour to Toye's diluted face, albeit momentarily. Houghton looked all over the horizon but could see nothing. His gaze moved from left to right and then ten yards in front of Geoffrey's sniper post where, finally, he saw a small movement on the ground.

'Hold your fire, Toye!' Houghton screamed. 'Hold your fire!'

Geoffrey carried on firing in a terrifying world that was his own. Losing his patience the captain grabbed the private by his coat and roughly dragged him from the top of the trench before throwing him to the floor. Geoffrey was stirred into the real world once more.

'Are you fucking deaf Toye?' he yelled. 'I said, hold your fire!'

'But I saw something, Captain,' replied Geoffrey, panting and shaking. Another flare flew into the sky. 'I saw something.'

'What did you see?'

'I couldn't see properly but something was moving out there.'

'Really?' He dragged Geoffrey up to his feet and pushed the periscope into his chest. 'Have a look! Have a fucking look!'

Geoffrey nervously climbed up the trench, peeped his telescope over the top and looked.

'Do you see it?' asked Houghton.

A scan of the ground revealed nothing.

'Well?'

Still, nothing. 'No, Captain but it must have…'

'Look again. Eleven o'clock about thirty yards away.'

Geoffrey looked once more and saw something moving on the ground. He took his eyes away from the periscope, rubbed them both hard and then looked again. Then he saw it; a huge rat stumbling wounded around no-mans land.

Geoffrey sighed, 'I see it, Captain.'

'Right Toye, come down.'

He slid down the sand bags of the trench wall. George and Morris, as well as the rest of the platoon, looked at each other in confusion.

'What was it, Private?' Toye mumbled inaudibly. 'I can't hear you, Private. What was it?'

Geoffrey swallowed. 'A rat, Sir.' Houghton raised his eyebrows. 'I mean, a rat, Captain.'

'A rat.'

'Yes Si.. Captain.' Sniggers came from the rest of the soldiers, but George and Morris were more concerned.

'A fucking rat!' Houghton stepped forward, right into Geoffrey's face. 'You wake me up in the middle of the night, you fire off rounds of valuable ammunition, you make me waste our last few flares and put the whole trench on alert, because of a fucking rat!'

Geoffrey's face dropped. He looked at his feet. 'Yes, Captain.'

'You're a fucking idiot, Toye.'

The Captain headed off down the line and told the platoon to get back to sleep. George and Morris looked at Geoffrey as sympathetically as they could. There was nothing they could say to ease the pain of the humiliation. Geoffrey began to cry and then headed off in the opposite direction.

'Geoffrey!' George shouted. 'Wait!'

The tearful private stopped, turned his head, showing half of his anaemic face, to half-glance at George. He seemed to stop as if to challenge George to say something. George failed and Geoffrey turned away again and headed off down the line of the trench.

George turned to Morris. 'Keep an eye on him.'

The air was thick with smoke; it hung around the lampshades of The Half Moon public house and weaved through the tankards hanging above the bar and through the hoards of men who crowded the little, dark room. Harry, followed by a slightly bemused-looking Ralph, politely shouldered his way through the bar. Ralph accidentally nudged an elderly gentleman whose beer spilled out of his tankard. The man turned around and before Ralph could apologise he grabbed him by the cheeks in both hands and planted a huge kiss on the composer's lips. Ralph was perplexed and didn't know whether to laugh or lose his temper. Before he had a chance to react Harry dragged him by the arm and pulled him to the far end of the bar. The genial barman wheezed at the pair.

'What will it be, gentlemen?'

'Two pint's of bitter please, mate,' said Harry.

The barman poured two frothing beers and popped them down on the bar. Ralph and Harry toasted their health with wry smiles and took a sip each.

'What are we doing here, Harry?'

'Well I understand that you have an interest in folk

music?' Ralph nodded. 'Well this is one of the best folk clubs outside of London, according to Mrs. Bloodworth.'

'Oh, I see.' Ralph looked and listened around looking for signs of music. 'That's splendid… where is it?'

'I don't know.'

Harry summoned the barman once again who directed the two to a long room at the back of the pub usually used for playing skittles. The friends found a seat in the corner of the room and made small talk for a while. Soon, two thin men arrived dressed in faded white shirts, waistjackets and flat caps, and sat down at the table next to them. They pulled out two fiddles and proceeded to tune their instruments. As strings were tightened and as the two instrumentalists practiced their scales Ralph's mind was taken back to a time when he would run up and down the same musical patterns with his viola teacher. A quick blink and a shake of the head and he was back. The two gentlemen began to play *The Wild Rover* and then a familiar tune, *Greensleeves*, played with energy and verve. As the evening progressed Ralph and Harry relaxed in the friendly surroundings of the folk club. They laughed and sang heartily through a host of familiar tunes. Ralph was struck by the professionalism of the amateur players. Not only were they able to play their instruments with technical mastery, they could also convey great emotion.

'What d'you think?' Harry asked.

'It's amazing!' said Ralph.

'I know their not as good as many of the musicians you are probably used to but…'

'No. I was just thinking that some of the musicians I have worked with could learn so much from these men.'

'What do you mean?'

Ralph expatiated. 'You see, music is both art *and* craft. It's the heart, but at the same time it's the brain.' Harry raised his eyebrows in need of more information. 'It's like a poem. Anyone can write a poem. They can find two words that rhyme and put them together, they might even use techniques like iambic pentameter, that's the craft. But to make the reader feel something – love, happiness, sadness, fear – that is the art. It is like putting your own mark on what you do. Craft is something than you can learn so that you can imitate a million others, art is something that you grow so that it can only be you. I have worked with some of the truly great musicians. They can memorise long passages of music and they can play the most demanding music without a single error. But they don't feel it. It's all in their head and in their fingers – but it's not in their heart.'

There was a moment of realisation. Harry looked at Ralph, lost in the honesty in his eyes and the passion in his voice, and a fire began to grow inside him. Then, without saying anything, he walked up to the musicians in the corner and whispered in an ear. The musicians struck up a chord and Harry pulled his harmonica out of his pocket. Harry launched himself into the opening notes of *Scarborough Fair*. As the melody drew to a close he sang the first lines of the song and within a moment more and more people in the dimly lit room were beginning to turn around and pay greater attention to the music. Soon hands were clapping the rhythms and enthusiastic sha-la-la's were punctuating and harmonising the tune until there seemed to be an orchestra playing, creating lush textures and filling everyone's heart with joy and merriment. Ralph was clapping along happily when Harry, in his wild excitement, beckoned him to join in with the musicians. Nerves and modesty prevented Ralph from running to participate, but in the end he succumbed to his friend's requests and made his way to the corner of the room. Harry, put his hands around Ralph and led the ecstatic audience in another round of singing. Ralph had never seen such informality in music. It had always been a very reserved affair since his first lessons through to the formality and etiquette of working with orchestras, chamber groups and choirs. The music continued long through the evening and Harry and

Ralph, for a moment, forgot that Britain was at war, or that they would soon be off to France to recover the dead and wounded. The only thing that mattered was the moment. By the end of the evening other local musicians had joined in on the accordion, the banjo, the guitar and two elderly gentlemen joined in - one playing the spoons, the other demonstrating the art of the paper and comb.

As they walked home the two friends talked only about music. The early February night showed the stars for all to see and the first signs of frost dusted the pavement enabling Ralph to see sparkles above and below. As they headed back to Mrs. Bloodworth's, wrapped up warm in their army issued coats, the subject of composition arose.

'So, why a composer?' asked Harry.

'I don't know really. I'm not sure I ever really chose it. My parents never pushed me, I never had a tyrant teacher or anything like that. It chose me, really. I don't think anyone who is creative, whether they are an artist, a poet, a sculpture or a composer ever really decides that is what they want to do. You just sort of grow into it. It just happens. You get this… need to say something. It might not be profound or earth-shattering but you feel it has to be said.'

'But why?' Harry placed his hands under his armpits to keep warm, 'I mean, other people – most people - just say it, or they just keep it to themselves.'

'Well maybe that's just it. I'm a reasonably intelligent man, I'm relatively articulate but there are some things I just can't say. I don't know why. But I *can* say it with melody, with harmony – with music.'

'I can't say I really understand.'

'I don't even understand it,' laughed Ralph. 'But, you're a musician you must have felt it.'

'What do you mean by *it*?'

'You know –*IT*?' Surely you have heard a piece of music or played something and it has… taken you somewhere. Somewhere else. Somewhere only you can go.'

'Like, where?' Harry's lack of insight seemed to be lightly testing Ralph's patience.

'Good grief!' Ralph looked up to the night sky and the two men stopped. 'It's almost… religious. When you hear a piece of Bach, it's like you're hearing something from another world, and if you close your eyes, as you listen, you *see* that other world.'

Harry took a good look into Ralph's eyes. 'You're a pompous old sod, aren't you?'

The two friends erupted with laughter and continued to do so as they continued to walk home. When the hilarity subsided Harry spoke again.

'No, it's really not that complicated to me. It's not anything high and mighty. Like tonight I wasn't taken to… to anywhere, I was happy where I was. It's as simple as that. Music makes me happy. Music is getting pissed with me mates, singing smutty songs in the pub. It's a good laugh that's all. That doesn't mean it's not important to me, that I don't… I don't appreciate it.'

'No, I'd never insinuate…'

'Because sometimes I s'pose I am taken to another place. But it's not music that takes me there; it's my boy or my wife. I can look at my boy and…Oh I don't know. I can't explain it.' He smiled wryly, 'Maybe I'm an artist after all!'

Ralph chuckled, 'Maybe!'

'Sometimes I look at my boy and I wish I could say it.'

'Say what?'

'Say how I feel. I suppose it would be nice at times like that to be able to write a poem or sing a song.'

'Then why don't *you* just say it?'

'I s'pose for the same reasons as you. I mean I'm not as educated as you -I'm not stupid, but I'm not going to go to Oxford that's for sure! Maybe the words just aren't there. Maybe that's why you write music. Some things can't be said or written, maybe they're just felt. I can't tell you how I feel when I look at my son.'

Ralph stopped his thought process for a minute and looked at Harry who, just for a moment had let go of his beguiling boyishness, and touched Ralph's heart. Then he smiled at his friend.

'Now who's pompous?' They laughed again.

## CHAPTER SIX

George had been awake most of the night. A chest infection had made sleep impossible. Every time he could feel the calmness of sleep encroaching, his throat and chest seemed to go into spasm. His head was pounding, like a timpani holding down a heavy, inescapable beat in his brain. Occasionally his coughing fits disturbed those around and he had to listen to the invective cries of disgruntled soldiers. As the daylight began to emerge George decided to rise and take a walk up and down the trench. At the far end of the line of slippery duckboards George noticed a movement. He moved closer to investigate. Something didn't seem right. He placed his hands on his revolver and tip-toed carefully forward. As he drew closer he realised that thankfully it was little more than a young Tommy private. Before he had a chance to greet the boy he began clambering over the British side of the trench. George rushed toward him and pulled him back onto the sandbags, his arms wrapped tightly around the boy. The private whimpered.

'What the hell are you doing?' George whispered.

'I'm g-g-getting out of here.' The boy struggled.

'Don't be stupid!'

'I'm not stupid. I'm not staying here to be b-b-b-blown to pieces.'

'So what? Are you going to risk court marshal? They'll shoot you.'

The boy struggled free. 'That's if they catch me.'

'They'll catch you alright!' said George.

'No, they'll be too b-b-busy worrying about the Germans.'

George grabbed the boy by the lapels and shook him. 'Think boy. Think! Do you really think they'll just let it lie? They'll make an example of you. If they don't then the floodgates will open and people will be deserting all over the bloody place.'

The boy started to cry. The tears welled up in his eyes and soon began to trickle down his muddy face. His tears were that of a terrified child who had woke up from a horrifying nightmare. The quiet madness quelled.

'What's your name?'

'Stanley. Stanley Anderson'

George took a deep breath which triggered yet another short fit of coughing.

'You do know that it is my duty to report this, don't you?'

'I know.' He wiped his eyes. 'Are you?'

George took a moment. 'No,' the boy swallowed in relief, 'but running off like this isn't going to help you. I promise you they'll find you.'

'I j-j-just can't….'

'I know,' George put his hand on the soldier's head and ruffled his hair kindly. The boy moved in closer and put his arms around George, who held him in return. 'It'll be okay. It will all be over soon. You mark my word.'

'I'm not so sure.'

'Where are you from, Stanley?'

'Penarth. It's a little t-t-town by Cardiff.'

'I know it,' George smiled. 'I used to holiday there with

my family. It's got a great big pier, hasn't it?'

'Yes.'

'We used to spend the day there, walk around, is it Alexandra Gardens?' Stanley nodded. 'Yes that's right - with the huge bird cage and the Zebra Finches. And then we'd go to Barry Island. Donkey rides on the beach.'

'Mum wouldn't let me go on them.'

'Why not?'

'In case I fell.'

'No!'

'Yes. Mum was… *is* very protective of me.'

'And yet she's fine with your being here?' Stanley sat up and raised his eyebrows sheepishly. 'She doesn't know you're here?'

'No.'

'Where does she think you are then?'

'I don't know.'

George took a moment to consider the enormity of the situation. 'How old are you, Stanley?'

'In the eyes of the army I'm eighteen.'

'And in your mother's eyes?'

He sighed. 'Sixteen.'

George rolled his eyes. 'Bloody Hell. How did you get through?'

'When I went to the recruiting office I lied about my age, didn't I?'

'And you told them you were eighteen.'

'No, I told them I was seventeen. I thought that was how old you had to be. The recruiting officer said to me, "Did you say eighteen, son?" I said, "No, I said seventeen." I remember him getting right into my face and saying, "I'm sure I heard you say eighteen." That's what he put on my form – eighteen.'

'Have you written to your Mother?'

'No,' said Stanley.

'Well, you've got to tell someone. You shouldn't be here.'

'No, I c-c-can't.' He cleared the tears from his eyes. 'I'll be punished.'

'By whom?'

'The army, my mother, my father – God.'

'So if you weren't going to go home, where exactly were you running to?'

'I don't know - anywhere but here.'

George coughed again and then held his head. The strain of his coughing was forcing his brain to pound harder still.

'Look, why don't you let me talk to your C.O. for you? Maybe we can work something out.'

'No, don't say anything, p-p-please.'

'Well, what do you want me to do?'

'Nothing. There's nothing you can do.' He stood up. 'There's nothing anyone can do.'

'There's always hope.'

'Not here, there isn't. Not big hopes.'

'Big hopes?'

'Yes, like hope you'll survive or hope that the war will be over soon. There are only little hopes.'

'Such as?' asked George.

'Little hopes like, "I hope the rats don't eat my rations," or, "I hope there's enough warm water for my tea."'

'Well then, hold on to the little hopes,' said George trying to smile. 'It's better than no hope at all. You'd better get back to your post before they start asking questions.'

Stanley picked up his belongings and nervously made his way back to his regiment. George watched him disappear down the line of the trench and started to cough again.

The morning was cold and crisp. A pale yellow sun hovered hopefully behind stubborn white clouds. Just as George was slipping into a gentle slumber while sat upright on sandbags he heard the harsh voice of Houghton shouting at his men.

'Morning inspection, gentlemen! Five minutes!' he yelled.

A flutter of activity ensued with men scurrying around looking for their equipment, adjusting their uniforms accordingly and washing the dirt from their faces. George organised himself and stood to attention outside a dugout. Standing opposite were Reggie and Geoffrey, the former looking tired, the latter looking worse. Houghton made his way down the line of the trench. The first few inspections were undertaken with minimal attention to detail. The main reason for the inspection seemed to serve no other purpose than to intimidate the soldiers. Houghton would stand almost nose to nose with the men as if to reiterate his authority. His walk was like that of a particularly strict headmaster, slow striding, hands behind his back and occasionally hovering threateningly. Then he came to Morris.

'Now then Private,' Morris saluted, 'let's have a look at you. Show me your small kit, soldier.'

'Yes, Captain.'

Morris pulled out a roll of leather and laid it out in his hands for Houghton to see.

'Now,' said the superior menacingly, 'do we have a spoon?'

'Check, Captain.'

'Knife?'

'Check, Captain.'

'Button stick?'

'Check, Captain.'

'Razor?'

'Check, Captain.'

'Shaving brush?'

'Check, Captain.'

'Bootlaces?'

'Check, Captain.'

'Good. Put it away, Morris.'

'Yes, Captain.' Reggie folded away the small kit and

once again stood to attention.

Houghton moved next to Geoffrey who was shivering in the freezing morning. His eyes were half closed, every now and then he would make a concerted effort to open them wider but the exertion only seemed to make him even weaker. He managed to salute Houghton.

'Now then, Toye. Show me your water bottle.'

'Yes, Captain.' From his belt he produced his water bottle and nervously presented it to the Captain.

'Thank you, Toye,' not a hint of sincerity. The captain examined the bottle. 'Oh dear! This appears to be empty, Toye.'

'Yes, Captain.'

'And why is that?'

'Please, Captain I have not been feeling well lately.'

'So you diagnosed your condition yourself and prescribed yourself some water, yes?'

'Yes, Captain.' Geoffrey struggled to stand still.

'Are you a doctor, Toye?'

'No, Captain.'

'No, Captain,' repeated Houghton sarcastically. 'So what will you drink when I send you over the top and you find yourself in a shell hole with your leg hanging off?'

Suddenly Geoffrey seemed to collapse inside. He knew that whatever he said, whatever he did, Houghton wanted to make him suffer. It was as though a weight had been lifted off his shoulders. He swallowed hard and plucked up as much courage as he could muster. Looking straight ahead he addressed the captain's question.

'Please, Captain, if my leg was hanging off I would imagine there would be a great deal of blood. Therefore I would use my water bottle as a receptacle to catch the blood and drink that in place of the water. I have heard that blood is quite nutritious.'

George and Reggie looked at each other incredulously. They feared Houghton's reaction. The captain took a step toward Toye, who now seemed to be regretting his new-found confidence, and smiled. Houghton then delivered a brutal head-butt right into Geoffrey's face. Reggie, standing alongside him, heard a crack and knew that his friend's nose was broken. He moved to help him.

'Leave him, soldier.' Reggie returned to his position. 'Up you get, Toye.'

Geoffrey stood upright and the whole trench could see the blood pouring from his nose. Geoffrey stood as still as he could and without making a sound looked Houghton squarely in the eye as the blood began to drip off his chin. The Captain took Toye's water bottle, removed the top and grinned at Geoffrey. Then, he undid his trousers, placed his penis on the top of the bottle and proceeded to urinate in it. As he did so he looked at Geoffrey, the blood still streaming off his face, and never once took his eye of him. With one hand Houghton pulled his trousers up and then put the top back on the water bottle, before placing it back in Geoffrey's holder on his belt. Then he took a step back.

'Clean that face up, you're a fucking disgrace.' The Captain walked off down the line. 'At ease gentlemen!'

Throughout that day Geoffrey kept well out of sight of Houghton. George didn't know what to do. Should he report the matter or would that make things even more uncomfortable for Geoffrey, and, for that matter, himself? He tried to talk to Geoffrey throughout the day but he was distant and unwilling to talk to George or, indeed, anyone. So, as night descended, George decided to sit down and write to Ralph. However, it was difficult to know what to say. To tell Ralph that he had seen dead bodies strewn over no-man's land, to tell him that he had watched rats gnawing and the bodies caked in mud, to tell him that he had witnessed the cruelty of Houghton and stories much worse would only serve to prove Vaughan Williams right. Also, all of the letters had to be censored and anything which told of a decline in morale would be unlikely to get through. Finally, George surmised that it would be too painful to relive such events anyway.

*Dear Ralph*

*I hope this letter finds you well. I wanted to write while I had the chance to say that I have witnessed real bravery today. I am not at liberty to divulge any details however I can tell you that what I saw would make you so proud of your countrymen. The Bosch is doing its level best to knock our spirits but despite the shelling and the gunfire they have failed. We spend our time laughing and joking and talking about the day when we can all come home. I have been doodling some musical ideas in my notebook and hope to have my first symphony completed sooner rather than later. Give my love to Adeline. Write back soon.*
*Your friend*

*George*

Although not proud of his untruths, George felt that the little white lies, as he saw them, were in everyone's best interest. He folded the letter and placed it in his pocket before leaning back into a small hollow dug into the side of the trench wall. He pulled his collar up over his shoulder and up to his cheeks. He closed his eyes and tried to block out the fading cries of, 'Wasser! Wasser! Bitte!' from a moribund enemy in no-mans land.

As sleep descended George found himself back on the beach in Hunstanton. The beach was completely empty. The sky above was grey and in his reverie George could feel the sea breeze on his neck. Everywhere was silent except for the waves kissing the shore gently in the distance. He was once again writing music in the sand only this time, rather than writing a short single melody, he had adorned the wet beach with a huge orchestral score complete with dynamic markings, articulation indications and sweeping phrase markings. He stood back and admired his work and began to conduct the music which ornamented the sand like some wonderful artwork. As he waved his arms and gestured to an invisible orchestra, he heard music playing so beautifully that he began to cry. As the melodies swayed back and forth and as the rich harmonies brought colour to the skies above he felt his heart rise and a tear of pure joy roll down his cheek. It was a moment of perfection, of beauty and innocence. Then, as he conducted, the sea came in closer, as it had in 1914, and the relentless incoming tide started to wash away the music. In his determination George continued to conduct. Yet, as the water rushed in it took away the music section by section. First to go was the woodwind section, followed by the brass leaving only the sombre strings. Eventually the music faded to the sound of a single double bass sounding before the cold waves came in and washed George's feet. At that moment George awoke to find that his foot had fallen into a huge puddle in the trench. He was panting slightly. The dream had not been a nightmare as such, however it wasn't particularly pleasant and the symbolism was not lost on George, as it wasn't on Ralph last year.

It was five in the morning and George needed to use the latrine, on his way back he heard gunfire. He headed back to his dugout and picked up his periscope. He cleaned the frost off the lenses and wiped them dry with his handkerchief. He peered through the lens and in the distance, with the imminent sun threatening the horizon, he noticed a single upright figure standing motionless in no-mans land. He wiped the sleep from his eyes and looked again. It was a young man tied to a post. His hands were tied behind his back and his feet secured to the foot of a stake driven deep into the ground. As the sun ascended, throwing light inch by inch over no-mans land, it illuminated the figure. George watched in morbid curiosity as the line of the sun crept up the man's feet, legs, waist and up past his stomach, chest and shoulders. Finally the rising sun threw light upon the face. To George's horror, it was a familiar face. It was Stanley. He had been shot to shreds by bullets seemingly from both sides. George looked away from the periscope, placed it on the ground and slowly headed back to his hole in the trench. Without blinking and without drama he looked at the wall of sandbags opposite and allowed a tear to roll down his cheek.

## CHAPTER SEVEN

The candle light flickered in the bedroom, illuminating Ralph's face softly but unevenly as he put pen to paper. Sat at a tiny desk by the window, with Harry snoring in one of the two single beds, once again he was completely blank. On the tabletop the manuscript paper was full of messy corrections and crossings out. Ralph screwed the paper up and threw it on a pile with the rest, and sighed. His exhalation was loud enough to disturb Harry from his slumber. He sat up in his bed.

'What was that?' he asked.

'Oh, sorry Harry, it was just me. I didn't mean to wake you.'

'That's okay,' he rubbed his eyes. 'What's the time?'

'It's just gone three.'

'What are you doing up at this time?'

Ralph bent down a picked up a handful of screwed up balls of paper and showed them to Harry, 'Composing.'

'Still struggling?'

'I just can't do it.'

'Well, I'm not surprised it's the middle of the bloody night.' He yawned, 'most people can't do anything in the middle of the night.'

'This is serious, Harry.'

'I'm sorry,' he could see that Ralph was particularly perturbed. 'Do you want to talk about it?'

'No, it's okay,' knowing full well he *wasn't* okay. 'I'm sorry.'

'No, that's alright.' Harry sat upright. 'Right let's try and look at this logically, shall we?'

'Why can't you write?'

'If I knew that I wouldn't be in this mess.'

'Okay, bad question!' He thought for a second, 'Well, what is stopping you writing?'

'I don't know. Nothing really – just me.'

'Well, what do you want to say?'

'I don't know. I'm not really sure I have anything to say.'

'Well maybe that's the problem.'

'What do you mean?'

Harry perched himself on the edge of his bed. 'Let's think about this. Why do people write?'

'I don't know.'

'Because they have something to say?' If you're *thinking* of something to say you're probably not saying anything at all, well nothing of any importance anyway. It seems to me that painters, poets, writers,' he smirked, 'even composers, only create anything once they are moved, or inspired by something. But you can't be inspired all the time, can you?'

'Go on.'

'Well, our lives are full of lots of inspirational things that can do strange things to the heart – sunsets, falling in love, watching nature, or whatever. But our lives are also full of the other... things. They're like the glue that holds all the special things together. So we also have to go to work, we also have to paint the windows, we need to milk the cows, cut the grass and all those other boring things. But you need those things so that the special things feel...'

'...Special,' added Ralph.

'Exactly. Does that make sense?'

'Sort of.'

'Okay, think of it like a telephone.'

'A telephone?' Ralph looked a little mystified.

'Yes. A telephone isn't always on receive is it?' Ralph nodded his head in confirmation. 'Sometimes it sends out doesn't it? It can't do both. I suppose creating is like a conversation with the rest of the world. You say something one day and then you listen. If you like, you are on receive. You have to spend time taking things in before you bugger around with them and put something new out.'

'So?'

'So you clearly haven't got anything to say at the moment. You are on receive right now. Just accept it.'

Ralph stood up and paced back and forth for a while. 'I can't. I can't just accept it. It's my job. If I don't write, I don't get paid.'

'You teach don't you?'

'Well, yes but…'

'But what?'

Ralph said nothing. He realised that his salary from teaching alone was more than enough to live comfortably on. He paced on, up and down the room.

'Anyway why haven't I got something to say? There are men, no, *boys*, sending themselves to France to be blown to pieces, the whole world is trying to bring itself to destruction and I have nothing to say.'

'Maybe you do have something to say, but you are afraid.'

'Afraid of what?' asked Ralph defensively.

'I don't know, I'm just posing the question. But you told me that you don't approve of the conduct of the war. Why wouldn't you speak out unless you were afraid?' He sighed. 'And there's nothing wrong with that. If you spoke out against the war, imagine what your audience would think? It's your career.'

'So what do I do?'

'There's only one thing you *can* do – wait.'

Training had been particularly grueling that day. As April said hello to 1915 the sun seemed to predict an early summer while the wind, which chilled from the north, echoed the remnants of winter. One way or another it didn't feel like spring. Training had been as repetitive as ever. Harry, Ralph's partner in class had wrapped imaginary wounds on almost every part of Ralph's body at least three times over. The instructor had talked them through particularly grisly eventualities. As such both Ralph and Harry knew exactly what to do with a soldier whose arm had been blown off, they knew how to approach a man cut to shreds by shrapnel or machine gun fire – in theory. In reality, who knew what might happen. So many unknown variables would come into play in the reality of warfare. Ralph had thought long about how he might cope in France. Would he freeze under the pressure? Would he make the correct decisions in the life and death split seconds he might have between encounters? Would he be able to euthenise those beyond saving? Classes were a daily grind of morbid make-believe, the Western Front, he felt, would be far worse than that.

As he met Harry outside the medical barracks to head home to Mrs. Bloodworth's warm hospitality, Ralph continued to grapple with his lack of creativity on one hand, and his apprehensions about his effectiveness in France. Harry arrived as he was in mid-thought.

'Penny for them,' he said with predictable amiability.

Ralph was stirred. 'Sorry?'

'You were miles away!'

'Oh, was I?'

'How about a beer tonight? If you like we could....'

As Harry continued talking, Ralph's attention was caught by the sound of a familiar, but at the same time unfamiliar, sound. It pierced the early evening air but seemed to be unnoticed by everyone else around - Harry continued talking and the other medics-to-be went about their business. It felt like the world had stopped turning for a moment as if pausing for a musical interlude. The music, as it was, was a bugle playing incompetently somewhere inside the barracks. The sound was shaky and inconsistent blows gave the instrument an uncomfortably thin timbre. The bugler was clearly trying to play an octave, but in his musical naivety he could only make an interval of a seventh. This two-note motif was repeated over and over. It hypnotised Ralph although he had no idea why. Musically it was awful, almost painful to the ears yet it somehow held his attention. For a moment Ralph was, metaphorically, somewhere else. Then the music stopped.

'... and then a pink elephant crawled into the bath with me and said, "hey nonny, nonny!"' The absurdities of Harry's words were enough to pull Ralph out of his daze.

'What?'

'I've been talking to you for about a minute.'

'Have you?' Ralph looked confused.

'Where were you?'

'Didn't you hear that noise?'

'What noise?'

'That music.'

'No, what music?'

'That bugle.'

'You really do need a beer tonight.'

'No, I mean it. I heard a bugle.'

'I didn't hear it mate. Sorry.'

Ralph walked off leaving Harry with his own confusion to deal with.

George, Geoffrey and Morris were sitting in the trench trying to throw little balls of dried mud into an empty can of bully beef. They were like school children playing marbles in the school yard. Occasionally 'ooh's and 'aah's would punctuate the game when a shot was particularly close. Then just as the game seemed to be drawing to a close, Morris noticed a rat on top of the trench wall. It perched itself on the sandbags and looked around curiously. Then it stopped for a while, seemingly frozen still. Morris nudged George who, in turn prodded Geoffrey for his attention.

'Ssshhh!' whispered Morris.

'What are you doing old boy?' asked Geoffrey under his breath.

'Sssshh!' repeated Morris, who, slowly and deliberately, picked up a large piece of mud, drew back and hurled the mud at the rat hitting it clean in the face. The rat scurried off while the friends exploded into rapturous laughter.

'You see Geoffrey, that's how you hit a rat!' laughed Morris.

As the sound of hilarity spread down the trench, others came to see what the commotion was about. Soldiers came by and listened as the three friends relayed the story to their peers. Soon there was a whole unit laughing and joking, and for moment there was real happiness in hell.

Houghton had heard the noise and came down the line to address the situation. He pushed his lanky frame through the crowds assemble around the three friends.

'What's going on here then, gentlemen?'

'We were just larking around, Captain,' replied Morris.

'Do you think this is the right place for larking around?'

'Oh, come on Captain,' said Morris, 'surely we are allowed to have a laugh every now and then.'

Under his breath Geoffrey mumbled. 'Miserable bloody sod!'

Houghton heard. 'What was that Toye?'

'Nothing sir… Captain.'

He moved threateningly toward Toye. 'No, it wasn't *nothing*,' he moved in closer. 'It was *something*.'

Geoffrey was intimidated but stood his ground. 'It was nothing Captain, really.'

Houghton stared at Toye menacingly. He looked up and down the Private as if looking for a weakness.

'Show me your gun, Toye.'

'Why do you want to see..?'

'Just do it, Toye.'

'What are you going to do?' asked Geoffrey nervously.

'Toye?'

'Yes, Sir… Captain.'

'It's very simple.' He stepped forward until he was almost nose to nose with Geoffrey 'Give… me… your… fucking… gun!'

Geoffrey reached to his side, his hands shaking, and withdrew his pistol from his holster.

'Thank you.' Houghton opened the chamber and smiled threateningly at Geoffrey. 'There is a bullet missing from your chamber Toye.'

'Yes Captain.'

'Why is that, Toye?

Geoffrey became nervous. 'I uh… I fired it a couple of days ago sir, I mean Captain.'

'You fired it.'

'Yes, Captain.'

'Why did you fire your gun?' He spun the chamber. 'Shooting rats again, were we?'

'No, Captain.'

'Then why did you fire your gun?'

'I thought I saw something approaching over the ridge yesterday. I thought it was the enemy.'

'And what was it?'

'It was nothing, captain it was my…' he swallowed anxiously. '…my mistake.'

'You do know that you should report any gun fire to your superior, don't you?'

'Yes, Captain.'

'Then why didn't you, Toye?'

'I don't know, Captain.'

Houghton stepped back a few paces and then turned around to Geoffrey while the rest of the men, including George and Morris looked on in trepidation.

'Well, I'm afraid this is a breach of army regulations. I should, in all fairness, deal with this as a disciplinary matter.' Geoffrey closed his eyes tight and then opened them as if trying to blink a nightmare away. 'Leave it with me, Toye.'

Houghton strolled away arrogantly leaving Geoffrey perspiring profusely, sharp prickles on the back of his neck as the hairs stood on end in fear.

Later that night George was sleeping in his familiar alcove of mud and water when he was disturbed by a movement just above his ankle. He half opened one eye and saw a small rat nibbling on his bootlaces. He nonchalantly kicked the rodent away, he was getting use to their presence. He was just about to resume his slumber when he heard whispering. It was Houghton. Five yards away the captain was kicking the feet of Geoffrey as he snored.

'Toye! Toye! Wake up!' Geoffrey stirred and rubbed his eyes. At first the sight of Houghton's cold, miserable face prompted him to think he was having a nightmare. No such luck.

'Get up!' he demanded. Geoffrey did so. 'Follow me, bring your rifle.'

George listened intently and watched again through a peeping eye. He watched as his friend followed the Captain down the line of the trench and round a corner of sandbagged walls. George picked up his own rifle and followed secretly, careful not to disturb the hoards of sleeping soldiers or the one or two night-shift snipers that surveyed no-mans land and the German lines behind. He made his way to the corner of the sandbags and peeped around. He could hear the conversation between Houghton and Geoffrey.

'Right Toye, I have a mission for you.' Geoffrey looked timidly at the Captain. 'Look over there, straight ahead, about thirty yards or so.'

Houghton handed Geoffrey a periscope, who rested

against the trench wall and popped the viewer over the top. He looked out over the desolation of the quagmire above and, due to the light of a particularly large full moon in the clear skies ahead, could see in relative detail.'

'You see that small mound of earth at eleven?'

'Yes, Captain.'

'Can you see a boot sticking up?'

'Yes.'

'Well that's Anderson. Bring him in.'

'But he's dead!'

'So?'

'Well it's not a rescue…'

'…No, it's a retrieval.'

'I don't understand.'

'Don't you think it would be… *honourable* for his family to have something to place in the ground?'

'But why do you want me?'

'Because I do?'

Geoffrey swallowed hard and clenched his fists hard. His mouth was drying up and he began to shake. George continued to spy around the corner. Geoffrey realised the malice behind Houghton's order and could feel the anger rising up inside him. He turned around, faced the trench wall and punched the sandbags hard. His lips were tight and his jaw muscles strained. He turned back to Houghton and took a deep breath.

'No!'

'What do you mean, "No"?'

'I won't do it. It's suicide. I'm not going out there just to let a sniper take a shot at me while I try to bring in someone who's already dead.'

'Are you refusing an order from your superior, Toye?'

'Yes I bloody-well am.'

'I could report you for this. I could put you on a charge of insubordination. Some might even see it as cowardice. Would you be prepared to face the firing squad?'

'You wouldn't.'

Houghton grabbed Geoffrey by the lapels of his coat suddenly. 'Just fucking try me!'

'Why are you doing this to me? Why me?'

'Because I will not be undermined or ridiculed in front of my own men by a sniveling fucking toff who's never had a speck of dirt under his nails.'

'Is that what this is all about? Money? You think I'm rich.'

'It doesn't matter what I think. You are going over that wall!'

'And if I refuse?'

'Then I'll kill you myself and throw your fucking body over there and you can join Anderson.'

'But I've got a family.' Geoffrey pleaded. 'I've got a little boy.'

'I couldn't give a shit if you've got fucking twins.'

Appealing to Houghton's humanity was clearly not going to work, he needed to be human first. Geoffrey could see there was no way out of his predicament other than to kill Houghton himself. He looked inside himself for moment but could see no cold blooded murderer. Houghton may have that ruthlessness but Geoffrey certainly did not.

George, still watching on was torn. Should he intervene and risk his own life or should he just hope that his friend would comeback from the battlefield alive? George watched as Geoffrey climbed the first few steps of the trench ladder, stopping half way to rest his head on a rung to say a prayer. He checked his rifle and then examined the chamber of his Webley revolver.

'Here's hoping you don't need that sixth bullet,' said Houghton showing no emotion whatsoever.

George watched as Geoffrey took in a deep breath of air and courage before climbing up over the top. The indifferent Houghton walked away down the trench, lighting a cigarette as he did so.

Geoffrey took his first steps in no-mans land but within

eight feet of the line of the trench he suddenly felt the warm sting of urine as it seeped into his clothes, then he felt nothing beneath him. All sensation in his feet and legs disappeared and he came crashing to the ground. There was no pain. There was nothing. He fell and rested his head in the mud for a moment and tried to manoeuvre his legs, but they were ridged and stiff. He hit them with his fists but could feel nothing. He wondered if he had been hit but could feel no wound, nor the wetness of seeping blood. He considered pulling himself back into the trench but knew what repercussions would await him if he did. He looked ahead and saw the marker of the mound of earth and the foot of Stanley Anderson sticking out of the ground. Laying on his stomach he began to drag himself quickly through the mire. A shot rang out in the distance and alarmed him so he quickly put his head down. He was uncertain as to whether the shot was aimed at him or merely stray gunfire. His heart throbbed and tears began to fall off his filthy face and into the mud. He continued to crawl forward with his face firmly in the dirt. As he reached out his hand he felt something hard and smooth. He picked it up to move it from his course, without looking, only eventually opening his eyes as he brought the object past his shoulder. It was a femur. It was stripped of all its flesh, no doubt by the rats and crows that feast on the human carrion generously littered all around. Geoffrey inhaled sharply then felt vomit rising from his gut. He was sick at once, then, acutely aware of the need to proceed quickly, he wiped the vomit and the thin strings of reeking saliva from his lips. He dragged himself along the ground quickly but it seemed to take an eternity to reach the small raised mound of mud he had spied from the trench.

George watched on in horror. He winced at Geoffrey's every movement. Every gunshot or shell, no matter how far away, made him shudder. As he watched he whispered the lines of the twenty-third psalm. When he came to the line, *Though I walk through the valley of the shadow of death, I will fear no evil, for thou art with me*, he repeated it over and over under his quickening breath.

As he drew nearer Anderson's corpse Geoffrey's breath kept rattling his vocal chords and he was unable to breathe silently. The more noise he made, the more he feared he might draw greater attention to himself and this only made him pant louder. Anderson's body was on its side, the spine facing Geoffrey as he approached. His hands still bound by the rope that once held him upright to the steak, half of which was still fastened to his upper-body. Geoffrey reached out and pulled the body towards him. Anderson's frame rolled over and as the moon shone down bright on them both Geoffrey saw the horrifying sight of Anderson's face. It crawled with maggots, the eyes had long been since eaten and the stench of the now disturbed rotting flesh was too much for Geoffrey to bear. He screamed, but this was not the scream one might hear when an icy hand touches the back of the neck in a darkened room. This was the scream of a thousand nightmares past and a thousand nightmares to come, a terror too unimaginable to put in to words, a sound which would forever stay with those who heard it. Geoffrey stared at the face as it crawled with decay, and the more he saw, the more the terror intensified. Yet he couldn't avert his gaze, it was as though he was hypnotised by its brutality, it was as though he had opened up a Pandora's Box and all of the world's evil, malice, ugliness, violence and depravity was staring back at him.

George looked through the periscope and heard Geoffrey's din. Without hesitation he climbed over the rim of the trench and began running through the mud to his friend. He yelled out to his friend and ran as fast as his sodden boots and weary legs would allow. As he ran he tripped over unrecognisable debris – barbed wire, shrapnel, corpses, body parts and guns which had become separated from their masters. It was only after the first few steps in no-man's land that George wondered what the hell he was doing, by which time it was too late. He had to carry on. The disruption of Geoffrey screaming in the middle of the night had alerted both parties into action. As George ran he started to hear gun shots and the sound of bullets whistling past his head like fireworks. In an attempt to confuse the German gunners, he zig-zagged his run in the hope that this might, at the very least, make the sniper earn his money.

Finally, he arrived in a muddy heap alongside the screaming Geoffrey. He took cover with his friend behind the mound of earth which protected them both from the barrage of bullets flying toward them.

'Geoffrey!' he called, yet his friend could not be disturbed from his madness. 'Geoffrey! Look at me!'

Finally, George was able to drag his friend away from his hysterical stare with the putrid corpse and get him to look into his eyes.

'Geoffrey! Look at me! It's just a dream. Give me your hand and we can wake up.'

Geoffrey looked into George's eyes and didn't seem to recognise him. His tear-filled stare seemed to look straight through him as he shook uncontrollably.

'We need to get out of here, Geoffrey. Now!'

'I c-c-can't move my legs.'

'Are you hit?'

'I-I-I don't think so. But I can't move them. They won't move.'

George thought for a moment. The bullets flew past the mound of earth which protected them and occasionally absorbed the blows before showering them with mud and dirt. Each hit nearby made them both cower deeper still, they seemed to dig themselves in deeper with each movement of their bodies, as though preparing their own final resting place.

'Right, we're going. Ready Geoffrey?'

With all the strength he could summon, George pulled his friend by the hand and began to drag him through the mud back toward the British trench. Geoffrey closed his eyes as tight as he could and waited for a bullet to hit. George stared at the British lines ahead, never taking his eyes off the uneven row of sandbags which constituted safety. Geoffrey felt the damp, cold mud at the bottom of his back as his belt line scooped up dirt as George pulled him along the ground. As George pulled his friend toward the trench, once again he quoted the 23rd Psalm under his quickening breath. Both could hear the sound of the bullets twisting through the air and felt dozens of tiny breezes where the closest shots passed. Geoffrey, unable to use his legs, tried as best he could to assist George by putting his hands into the mud, using them like surrogate feet and running with them. As they approached the British line George feared the bullets of his own men returning fire and in the confusion and terror this was not wholly unjustified. Finally they reached the sandbags. George stood up and swung Geoffrey over the sandbags and into the trench. As he did so he felt a thud on his shoulder which spun him round and catapulted him on the sandbags, followed by a searing hot pain. He let loose a deafening yawp then managed to roll over the trench wall and down on to the duckboards below. Geoffrey, already at the bottom of the trench on his stomach was shivering and shaking frenziedly. George, lying on his back next to him, could feel the warmth of his own blood seeping from his shoulder into his mud-caked uniform. He took in a huge gulp of air and passed out.

Consciousness came first with noise. George was aware of the busy sounds of nurses and surgeons running around him. He heard the chaotic calls of doctors for help and the moans and cries of soldiers in agonising pain. Resting on his back, he opened his eyes slowly and saw the sun creeping through the criss-cross fabric of a canvas tent. He squinted his eyes until they were almost shut and the light seemed to sparkle. The tighter he closed his eyes the longer the shafts of light became. For a moment he wondered if these were beams of light from heaven. He lifted his head and scanned the room. The clearing station was full of lamentable distortions of humanity – grown men calling for mummy while nurses and doctors tried to hold their intestines within their blood-drenched torsos, young privates being held down by medics while shrapnel was removed from legs and arms without anesthetic. He heard a doctor passing by his bed in conversation with a nurse.

'Bed number five – there's nothing we can do,' he said in a respectable upper-class accent. 'Get his details while you can.'

'Yes, Doctor.' replied the nurse.

George looked around his bed to see if he was in bed number five but there was no indication of number on his bed. As he looked around he saw a man beside him on the floor to his left, his face covered with a blanket and a mutilated arm poking out from underneath. George turned his head away quickly and to his right he saw a man who was seemingly in good health.

'Where are we?' he asked.

The man, lean and handsome in his late thirties, stared at George vacantly, showing no sign of recognition or emotion. When George asked again he stirred slightly and tried to speak, but his lips moved without sound. He tried again but once more was silent. The mute lay back down and turn on his side away from George.

'Geoffrey!' he cried. 'Geoffrey!'

He fell back down, closed his eyes and tried to believe he was dreaming. Within a couple of heartbeats darkness descended.

Being billeted in Bishop's Stortford was beginning to irk Ralph. That evening not even Mrs. Bloodworth's heart-warming hospitality could stop Ralph descending into a spiral of boredom and frustration. Still unable to write, he passed the nights away by reading but he had read everything to hand and so was excited when Mrs. Bloodworth popped her smiling face into his room and deposited a letter which had arrived earlier that day.

*Dear Ralph*

*I cannot lie, the last few weeks have been most trying. The war just seems to keep on taking. It starts with your sense of humour. The strange and quirky nuances of good men, which at first could make one smile, soon become over-familiar and tiresome. Then it takes your sleep, and when it hands it back to you in the form of forty winks in the dug out, you wish it hadn't. Nightmares come regularly to me. I see the men whom I have killed – they don't do anything, they don't say anything they just stand there, as if waiting for a reaction. They are pale and dressed in British uniform. I dare say that Austrian chap would have a field day analysing the sum of my slumber. Then the war takes your strength, until you can hardly lift your rifle. Finally, it takes your health. Without your strength you can't fight off infection like a cold or flu.*

*Geoffrey is on his way back home and may even arrive before you receive this letter. He has had a tough old time. The incessant barrage of gunfire and shelling has apparently had an erosive effect on his wits. Although physically he is fine he is unable to walk. I understand the condition is known as war neurosis. So now, it seems, the war has taken Geoffrey – or at least the best of him.*

*But there are two things that the war has not, and will not take away – my hope and my faith. If I lose those things, if **we** lose them, then we will count the dead not in thousands - but millions. I know your faith follows a different path to mine yet we both long for the same things – peace, justice, love and, above all, an end to all of this.*

*I will concede to you one thing; this war is like no other before it. I have seen in recent months the cruelty that mankind can inflict but I have also seen the beauty of men too. Even here in hell beauty can exist, you just have to look a little harder.*

*Keep looking and keep the hope!*

*George.*

# CHAPTER EIGHT

1916

The longest day of the year was a blessing of beauty and, as such, Ralph and Adeline walked the gardens at Sandringham, and took in as much of it as they could. The last day of his short period of leave, before finally heading for France, had to be savoured. The simple things seemed so perfect. Yes the rhododendrons, vibrant in their purple hues caught his eyes; yes, their scent drifted through the air and romanticised his nose with each inhalation; and yes, the June sun made their loveliness all the more perfect. But beauty could be found elsewhere. Ralph noticed a host of dandelion weeds among the grass verges that ran along side the footpath through the forest. He picked one up and looked at it closely. So many times he had pulled them up from his lawn and been indifferent to their complex, yet delicate, beauty. This time he saw the white, fibrous taraxacum seeds as he had never seen them before. Each seemed like the skeleton of an umbrella, its outstretched spokes reaching for the wind, soon to be carried away to the uncertainty of the world. He blew the seeds gently into the air and watched them catch the breeze. There was particular a poignancy for Ralph who could not help but watch the moment metaphorically. For a second he saw hundreds of tiny soldiers floating silently away through the forest but he blinked them away. Life seemed so fragile.

That afternoon Ralph and Adeline rested beneath the shade of the tall pine trees in a clearing in the forest. They had managed to escape the hoards of summer revelers and had found their own little Eden. The profound nature of each and every moment was not lost on the two lovers. Although neither would have believed it possible, they both found themselves falling deeper in love with each other. Each kiss seemed more and more tender, and tasted sweeter than ever. Ralph held Adeline's delicate white hands and they seemed so soft and light that at times he wondered if he held them at all. Every utterance was musical. Adeline's soft tones were lyrical and at a time when creativity had deserted him, Ralph, at that moment, felt he could write the perfect melody. He savoured so many potential finalities. Each time Adeline placed her hand inside Ralph's shirt to lovingly caress his back he wondered if it would be the last time he would feel her hands there. Every time she looked at him a certain way he would try to commit the image to memory, so that he might build in his mind a sketchbook of her face; something beautiful to call upon in the ugliness of France. Ironically, as he sat on the train later that day, having kissed Adeline for the last time and waved goodbye from King's Lynn station, he could remember hardly anything.

There were a few last minute chores to do before leaving for France. As well as buying a gift in town for Mrs. Bloodworth, to thank her for her kindness, Ralph also wanted to visit Geoffrey. He was recuperating in St Albans at the Middlesex War Hospital which, formerly an asylum, now aided the recovery of those suffering the various forms of war neurosis. He took the early train west with the view to purchasing something in St Albans and seeing his friend in hospital, thereby killing two birds with one stone.

Outside the train station was a small gift shop which provided Ralph the opportunity to buy Mrs. Bloodworth a fine bone china cup and saucer for her now legendary cups of tea. The helpful young lady, Ralph suspected, was earning a little extra money above her real job as a munitionette, on account of the yellow tinge to her lovely skin. She wrapped the gift carefully in brown paper and placed it in a small, wooden gift box safe for the journey home.

A little later, Ralph made his way to Napsbury Park and within the splendid greenery of a host of summer trees he saw the hospital. It was a large imposing building with a huge clock tower above the reception entrance, commanding views over the large lawns and meticulously maintained gardens which surrounded. As he approached he saw nurses aiding men walking with all manner of contortions and distortions. Others were being pushed in squeaking wheelchairs. Occasionally, there would be a loud scream and orderlies would rush frantically to the source of the din.

Ralph disconcertedly made his way to the reception area. He stood on the black and white tiled floor and took in the enormity of the building, its high ceilings and stone marble columns. He made his way to the front desk to enquire after Geoffrey. An orderly showed Ralph to the far end of the building, down long corridors empty of visual stimulation, to a garden of white and yellow roses. In a wheelchair on a patch of lawn Geoffrey sat with his hands in his lap. Ralph made his way to his friend and shook him warmly by the hand. He wanted to hold his friend tightly but nervousness and Englishness ensured a far more formal greeting than either was particularly comfortable with.

'Geoffrey, it's good to see you.'

'Good to see *you*.'

Ralph looked at his friend, his legs almost completely straight in front of him, unable to bend or reach the floor. 'How are you?'

'Well, I'll need a runner in cricket for a while,' he smiled, 'but I think I could probably bat okay.'

An awkward silence ensued. 'It's a nice place here.'

'On a day like today, yes. It's nice to be outside away from the *real* loonies.'

'What do you mean?'

'Well, put it this way I am one of the least afflicted.' He shuffled uncomfortably in his wheelchair, 'I share a room with a man called Bryson. He's a dear fellow from Cornwall. Very clever too. To look at him you wouldn't think there was anything wrong with him. But at night at the slightest bang, like the closing of a door down the corridor, or someone slamming the window downstairs, he screams, jumps out of bed and runs into the closet where he proceeds to… to urinate and defecate. You can hear the whole thing happening, you can see the closet shuddering and then you get the smell. Sometimes it's set off by a nightmare.'

'Good lord! And you?'

'I have my own nightmares.'

'What are they?'

Geoffrey paused. 'They are *mine*.'

Unwilling to pursue the subject of bad dreams any further, Ralph changed the subject. 'Have you heard from George or Reggie?'

'Not for a while. The last I heard, Reggie was hooking up with another regiment at the second Ypres. I used to think no news was good news, but I'm not so sure now. He was still writing something or other in the trenches before I left – a string quartet I think.'

'And George?'

'He had a spot of leave which he declined.'

'Why did he decline?'

'He said he wouldn't leave his men.'

'*His* men?'

'Yes, didn't you hear?'

'No.'

'He was promoted - commissioned to second lieutenant with the 13th Battalion, Durham Light Infantry.'

'Good grief!'

'That's not all.'

'No?'

'No, look at this.' Geoffrey handed Ralph a copy of the morning paper and pointed to a section at the bottom. 'Read that.'

Ralph read through the dispatches about George's bravery in a trench raid. 'Good Lord! He's been recommended for the Military Cross!'

'Yes,' said Geoffrey proudly.

Ralph turned his back on his friend and silently walked away. He ran his fingers through his hair and then looked up at the perfectly blue sky. Geoffrey was concerned.

'Ralph? What is it?'

'What the bloody hell does he think he's doing?'

'He's a soldier Ralph, more than that, he's a leader. He's doing what soldiers do. What they *have* to do.'

'He should be keeping his head down, the silly fool.'

'Now hang on old boy, he's…'

'… Going to get himself killed,' interrupted Ralph angrily.

'I was going to say, he's not stupid. He's not on some machismo suicide mission.'

'Well, he could have fooled me.'

'You fool yourself Ralph. If you can't see that he's doing it for you, if you can't take just a second to appreciate what he's done, if you can't… If you can't just be proud of him, then you are the fool.'

Geoffrey swung his chair around and wheeled himself off down the garden. Ralph put his hands in his pockets. He was furious with George but now more so with himself.

He watched Geoffrey head off down the garden. As he came to a dip where the lawn met the patio he struggled to negotiate his way safely. Ralph went over to help.

'I can manage you know,' he snapped. 'I'm not an idiot.'

'I never said you were, old boy. I'm sorry.'

Geoffrey sighed. 'Me too,' he wheeled around to face Ralph. 'I didn't mean to bite your head off.'

'No, I deserved it.'

'I know why you are *really* angry with George.'

'Oh? Tell me.'

'You love him.' Ralph smiled uneasily. A red mist of embarrassment seemed to fill his cheeks. 'And there's nothing wrong with that.'

'No?'

'Certainly not. You see we learn about love between men and women, we're taught it – Romeo and Juliet, Cupid's arrow, Eros and all that stuff. But love between men is considered… well, strange, somehow wrong. I know it happens out in France. Strangers become friends, friends become… more than friends. Then things get physical. But love is physical. In a place where there are no women, is it any wonder that a man might look to another for something… tactile? But that's not the love you have for George. Yours is a caring pastoral kind of love, but no less poignant or touching.'

Hearing these words the birth of a tear began to well up in Ralph's eyes. However, with typical English stoicism and reservation, he fought them back with a swallow and a cough.

'But even now you can't let go of your Englishness.'

'Well I am English.'

'And you're also a human being. Don't let your Englishness come between you and your humanity.'

Geoffrey showed his friend around the rest of the gardens.

Ralph was of the opinion that this was not a place of pastoral or medical treatment, rather a workshop where fighting machinery was repaired with the view to send it back to active service. There was care, but nothing personal. Nobody was on first name terms and the healing was done coldly and pragmatically. The only thing that mattered was getting these men, wherever possible, to go back to France. Geoffrey told Ralph about the treatment he and others had received. He spoke how some of the mutes, mostly lower rankers like privates and corporals, were often sent to London to receive treatment from Dr Lewis Yealland, a Canadian neurologist who treated, and cured *all* of his patients with electricity and metal oral probe. Ralph shuddered as he heard how the patients would be strapped into a chair, their mouths forced open and then a strong electric shock would be delivered right onto the larynx. Ralph also heard about Dr William H Rivers in Edinburgh. His method were more time-consuming but less brutal than Yealland's. He believed that mutism or psychoparalysis came as a result of repressed memories. Through discussion and, sometimes hypnosis, the patient would be taken back to the moment when the shellshock first appeared. In essence the mind was eroded by the onslaught of guns, shelling and the general hysteria of the trenches and would begin to shut down.

'So what happened to you?' asked Ralph as they made their way round to the front of the hospital.

'Human nature happened.'

'What do you mean?'

Geoffrey paused for a moment and looked vacantly into the distance. 'I heard a story about a young lad called Mellor. He was eighteen, just. He was ordered to take part in a trench raid by his captain. He stood at the foot of the trench ladder and was given the order to move out. He went to climb the ladder but his top half seemed to move alone. His legs were completely frozen. He couldn't move them. He began to pull himself up the ladder by his hands and then his hands became rigid. They couldn't free his grip. He was stuck to the ladder. They shot him for cowardice. He was no more a coward than me. My legs stopped at the top of the ladder, if they had stopped at the bottom, I'd have been sat on a chair with a blindfold over my eyes. It's simple human nature. We're just animals really. We avoid danger. We run from death. Your superior tells you to walk into a wall of bullets, your brain – your human nature - tells you to run in the opposite direction. Standing still is the compromise.'

Those last few words ran around Ralph's head for the rest of the day. On the train they kept repeating themselves over and over again, to the point where he almost blocked out the incessant crying of a spoilt toddler who had been refused a toffee apple by his mother before setting off. *Standing still is the compromise.* He considered the military situation on the Western Front. For nearly two years the German and British armies had in effect been standing still, better that than to have the Kaiser's troops storming throughout England – a compromise. The battle plans of both parties seemed to be defensive and as a result thousands of troops along the line of trenches had stood still, stuck in the mud due to the political incompetence of their leaders. Ralph also viewed Britain as standing still; neither she, nor her empire, could continue to develop their hold on world of commerce until the war was over. His marriage would stand still while he undertook his military obligations, as would his career and his relationship with George. Most concerning to Ralph however, was the stagnation of his creativity. Beside the recurring bugle melody which seemed to play over and over in his head, like a scratched recorded bouncing back and forth on a gramophone, nothing of any creative value had been forthcoming. The melodies that once accompanied his every step were now silent; the rhythms still, the harmonies empty. Beside the financial concerns that this loss of creativity might bring, he worried that he might go through the war without being able to offload the feelings and thoughts which would undoubtedly accost him from time to time. Following his meeting with Geoffrey earlier that day he knew that the images in his mind of England's rolling hills, innocent lambs frisking in scenic meadows and skylarks playfully singing their tuneful calls through summer skies, would soon be replaced, or at least overshadowed, by images too terrible to imagine. The only way he knew how to face his demons was through music. He knew that he was not particularly adept at expressing his emotions through conversation, and the thought that he might *never* talk of his experiences in war was more than a distinct possibility. He feared that all the ugliness of the war might claim dominion over his mind and, without creative outlet, would fester and simmer inside him for the rest of his life. However, at least he would never be given a white feather and he could forever say that he did his duty – that was his compromise.

'Penny for them,' said Harry as Ralph looked out beyond the wooden railings on deck of the SS Inventor as it headed across the English Channel.

'I was just recalling my last experience on the sea,' said Ralph leaning over the barrier and looking at the wild waves below. 'I'd been out swimming on the south coast and got into trouble. The current was pulling me this way and that way, up and under, and I thought that my time was up. I kept taking mouthfuls of water, I could hardly see where I was, I couldn't get my bearings. There was no point trying to swim. The best I could do was to try and hold my breath long enough for the current to carry me somewhere safer. I was completely helpless. There was *nothing* I could do. In the end I was washed onto some rocks and managed to get a grip and pull myself ashore. I was lucky. George said that God had been watching me and had guided me ashore. I told him that it was God that put me there in the first place.'

'The lord giveth and the lord taketh away,' said Harry in his most pompous voice.

'I wish he'd make his bloody mind up!' The two friends laughed at their religious irreverence like two misbehaving schoolchildren telling jokes at the back of a classroom.

During the remainder of the journey the two friends laughed as though they were day-tripping to Yarmouth rather than heading for the front line. Harry told tasteless jokes which Ralph did his best not to enjoy but frequently found the hilarity undeniable. They sang songs, Harry played harmonica and the two of them did whatever they could to enjoy life while they were able.

The landscape was desolate. Charred skeleton trees rose from the mud indeterminately – not even mother nature, it seemed, had been spared in this war.

'Welcome to Ecoivres,' said a tired Canadian voice as Ralph, Harry and a host of other medical personnel stepped off the wagon near Vimy Ridge.

'Bloody Hell!' said Harry staring into the wastelands. 'Where are we?'

'You are about five miles north of Arras, mate,' said the medic, a squat man in his late forties with little colour in his face. 'You the new boys?'

'Yes,' said Ralph.

'Well let's show you around, give you a tour of Vimy ridge.'

As they wandered through the mud Ralph and Harry were silent. There was little to say. The mud had been liquidised into a sticky sludge by uncharacteristically heavy summer rains and Ralph could feel a vacuum in the ground pulling at his feet, making each step an effort. By the makeshift clearing centre, which was little more than a brown canvas tent with a red cross darkened by mud on a white background faded by filth, he watched as ambulance drivers and medics carried in the covered corpses of soldiers recently deceased. He watched as they were laid down in rows beside each other. They almost seemed to disappear anonymously into the wet earth beneath them while medics and soldiers from Britain and Canada marched by indifferently. Ralph was more than aware that those lying dead on the ground were fathers, sons, brothers, uncles and cousins. But this was no place for sentiment. He watched in disbelief as an English soldier lifted the sheet covering one of the dead and frisked his mutilated body for military seconds. He took the soldier's water bottle and knife and placed them in his jacket. Harry, also seeing this was incensed, and in fury he ran toward the soldier and punched him firmly in the jaw, sending him flying into the mud.

'You fucking bastard!' he seethed. 'You piece of shit!'

Harry piled on more punches while the soldier cowered beneath the blows, covering his head with gaunt skinny hands. Ralph ran over and with the help of the other new recruits managed to ply Harry off the terrified soldier. As Ralph held Harry back the soldier made his way nervously to his feet.

'You're a fucking parasite!' yelled Harry. 'Why don't you show some respect. That's someone's son and all you can do is rob him.'

The soldier safe in the knowledge that his assailant was now restrained plucked up the strength to reply,' He's dead you idiot! What does a dead man need a water bottle for? He's dead for Christ's sake.'

'You bastard!' Harry tried to struggle free but Ralph held on tighter.

'It's a basic use of resources. I'm going to take whatever I can get hold of to keep me alive out here, anything to stop me ending up like them,' he pointed at the row of corpses.

'Don't you bloody care?'

'Of course I fucking care, you idiot. But I also care

about *my* son and I'll do anything to make sure that I see him again.' Harry simmered and Ralph loosened his grip. 'Of course I care. I mean, what do you want me to do? Burst into tears every time I come across a dead soldier? You do that here and you are as good as dead.'

Harry considered a response but how does one respond, he thought, to the undeniable? Slowly and mournfully he moved back to the disfigured body on the ground, pulled the sheet back over his face, it was the only dignified thing he could do. Ralph watched with concern as Harry walked off toward the clearing station with his hands in his pockets and his face firmly fixed on the ground.

*My Dear George*

*Today I arrived in France and witnessed first hand the results of this war. I know not what it will do to me, only what it has done. Today has made me even more cynical – if that were possible. I saw my first dead body today and I don't quite know how it has affected me. I feel strangely numb. Am I repulsed? Yes. Am I angry? Of course. But all of these feelings seem to be trapped within what Geoffrey would call "overt Englishness." It's like I am trying to hold on to some wild animal. The more I hold onto it, the more furious it becomes before eventually it breaks free and lets all of its animal instincts loose. Tomorrow morning we will undertake our first shift. I cannot deny that I am most terribly nervous, but my fear is for my mind rather than my body.*

*Geoffrey tells me that you have been recognised for your bravery. I congratulate you but please, I implore you – be careful! There is a fine line between bravery and recklessness.*

*Your ever devoted friend*

*Ralph*

*P.S. Geoffrey passes on his regards, I have yet to hear from Reggie.*

# CHAPTER NINE

The road to Pozières had taken its toll on the legs and feet of those in the Durham Light Infantry, including George but in his new role of Lieutenant. He would keep his pain to himself and first consider the plight of his men. In the mid-morning summer sun the company stopped at one end of the Albert-Bapaume Road which led to a ridge occupied by the Germans in the centre of the town. George gathered his men together and told them all to sit down and remove their footwear. One by one he inspected the feet of his soldiers and ordered those with particularly horrid blisters to have the medic look at them and dress them. Such care for his men had made him a popular leader. George's new captain, a muscular Yorkshire man, with black hair parted flatly down the centre, Edward Burnham, was a determined yet amiable man. He had been impressed with his lieutenant and recently had recommended George for further mentions in dispatches for the brave example he had set his troops during a trench raid. He watched once more in admiration as George tended to his blistered corporals and privates.

'Right Thomas,' he said cheerfully, 'let's have a look at you shall we?'

'Thank you, sir,' said the young private, removing his hat and wiping his brow beneath a fringe of sweaty blond curls. 'It's my toes really. My heels are uncomfortable but I'm not going to moan about them, I can cope with them.'

George pulled apart the private's toes. 'Oh! That looks rather nasty, young man.'

'Oh!'

'Yes, your toes are a real mess. It's a wonder you were able to walk at all. The one on your heel isn't great either. Right, I want the medic to have a look at you.'

'Yes, Lieutenant.'

'Anything else you need?'

'Well, a nice scotch wouldn't go amiss, sir,' joked the teenager. 'If you're paying that is, sir.'

George flicked Thomas's ear playfully. 'Watch it you!'

George continued his foot inspection until all of the corporals and privates had been seen before heading back along the road to a spot beyond the view of his company. He sat down and removed his own shoes and socks and winced painfully. He carefully separated the toes on his right foot and saw red raw flesh. Wet with sweat and the fluid from burst blisters, he waggled the foot to allow the air to begin the healing process. It was agony, but George had learned how to control pain the way he learned to control his fear – by giving it no recognition. He took out a small flask of whiskey which Captain Burnham had surreptitiously sanctioned and took a small sip before trickling a little on to his open wounds. As the rush of pain surged through his body he tightened his lips, inhaled deeply and then held his breath for a while before exhaling. For a few moments he rested on the ground and felt the breeze weaving through his stinging toes.

After his brief respite George was summoned to a meeting with Captain Burnham.

'George, dear boy,' he said. 'We've received our orders.'

'Yes sir?'

'We are to support the Anzac attack on Pozières. If we take the second German line – or the OG line – as it's known.' George looked puzzled. 'The Old German line.'

'I see, Captain.'

'If we take the town and the ridge it rests on we'll not only put a few Bosch away, but we'll also be able to take the vantage point from which to monitor the whole area.'

'When is the attack, sir?'

'That's the thing,' said Burnham, wincing while smoothing his pasted black hair. 'They want to move tomorrow. Early morning -just after midnight in fact.'

'But we've only just arrived.'

Burnham looked his file. 'Oh no, I lie, we set out at 1:30 am. Yes I know it's hardly ideal.'

'But the troops are in no state to move anywhere at the moment. They're tired and half of them can hardly walk on account of their blisters, sir.'

'This is a war, Butterworth. It's never going to be ideal. It is what it is. Anyway, I'm sure you can motivate them. They'll fight for you if they'll fight for anyone.'

'Thank you sir,' George swallowed, 'but, with respect, I can't see how we can get the best out of these men while they're in this condition. They're a good bunch, stoic and brave but in their state… I don't feel that…'

The Captain interrupted, '…I don't care what you feel, Lieutenant. No body cares about what *I* feel. Feelings don't come into it; we have a job to do.'

George submitted, 'Yes sir.'

Burnham relinquished his formality for a moment. 'You're a good man, George - one of the best. And you have good men too. But this is a bad war, and this is as good as it gets.'

Later that evening on the road side near Pozières George was only certain of one thing; that the late July sun would fall in the west. He set up a fire and boiled some water for tea for his men. He pulled together the company and spelled out the battle plans. There were sighs but no complaints from anyone. Around the fire each soldier checked his equipment. Guns were oiled, knives and bayonets were sharpened and each was issued with a Mills grenade. Supplies were prepared and each soldier made sure that their medical kit was in order.

'I would also suggest that you sharpen your razors gentlemen,' said George wandering fatherly through his men as they sat on the roadside. 'It might come in handy.'

George noticed Private Boon, a twenty-something from Leeds, weeping quietly and discretely into his hands. He wandered over to him and ruffled his hair. He bent over and placed his own head on Boon's.

'Come on, Boon. You'll be fine.' He stood up and addressed the rest of his men. 'We'll all be fine! If we all stick together, concentrate and don't do anything stupid we'll all get a period of home leave.'

'Do we know how many Germans are up there?' asked a tall, gangly Corporal Emerson.

'Enough.' George shrugged his shoulders. 'Enough to keep us busy for a while. But the Australians and New Zealand lot are a strong bunch and together we'll do it.'

George noticed that heads were beginning to drop, tears were beginning to fall and hands which tried to load pistol chambers were beginning to shake.

'Listen up everyone!' he said, 'Who likes music?'

There was a muted response. They soldiers looked around at each other in confusion.

'Come on!' he urged, 'Who likes music?'

At last, a couple of hands were raised and more than a few heads nodded.

'I am a composer,' said George. 'I'm a musician. I write music.' The personal insight into their superior's life made the group curious and attentive. 'I have been working on a Symphony. I have it right here in my note book, well, bits of it at least.'

'Are you famous?' asked the blue-eyed Private Millar as George got out his note book to show the troops.

'Had you heard of me before?'

'No, Lieutenant.'

'Then no – I'm not famous.'

'But you might be some day, Sir,' added a goofy but likeable Private Harford.

'Well yes, maybe, but that's not what it's about is it?'

'Why not?' badgered Harford.

'Because it's about the music. I don't want to be famous, I want the *music* to be famous.'

Harford came back once more, 'But if you're famous you get your name in the paper.'

'Yes and that's the last thing I want!'

'And you could be rich,' added the barely broken voice of Private Gulley.

'Well, I wouldn't mind that,' laughed George before pausing. 'But tonight as *I* try to get some sleep I will listen to music in my head. I hear Bach and Mozart, maybe a little Brahms.'

'Beethoven?' asked Millar.

'Of course.'

'But he's German,' noted a beefy Corporal Johnson.

'*Was* German, Johnson. He's been dead for nearly ninety years. And anyway nobody's perfect.'

'What about Tchaikovsky?'

'Less so.'

What about that bloke, what's his name? Williams.'

'*Vaughan* Williams,' added Millar. 'He's the one what wrote that Tally Thomas thing.'

'Thomas Tallis, you berk!' said Johnson.

George paused for moment and in the blink of an eye he found himself in Ralph's study in Sherringham. He could feel the warmth of the flames as they crackled in the fire place. The two of them were sat side by side at the piano playing folk tunes while Adeline bowed her cello. He could hear the joyful melodies sliding and gliding through effortless key changes. He could taste the fine wine on his lips and smell the scent of beef simmering in herbs and onions in the kitchen. It was a moment of complete and unadulterated happiness.

'Sir?' asked Millar. 'What about him? What about Vaughan Williams?'

George stirred and then smiled. 'Yes, I'm sure I'll hear him. You see good art, whether it's the Mona Lisa or Thomas Tallis, is important because it reminds us of the divine. It proves that there is a God and that he is capable of such beauty, while we are capable of such ugliness. Great music reminds us of the eternal life because what is beautiful now, will be beautiful forever. And all that music that can make you cry, that makes you laugh, makes you proud, makes you angry, makes you contented – can also make you strong.'

The troops were hanging on George's every word as he delivered his speech deliberately and passionately.

'Now,' he added, 'when we get out here – and we *will* get out of here – I will write my first symphony and dedicate it to each and every one of you in person. What's more I will invite you all to attend its premier as my guests, because I can think of no finer men to share an evening with. Now, get some rest.'

As George walked away from his men he heard three cheers strike up in his honour. He turned around to the men, smiled proudly and walked on. As he headed off into the fading light he felt sure that he had given the men honour, but had he given them hope? And if so, was it any more than false hope? Finally, he found a place on the roadside away from anyone and considered what he had said. He began to undertake his own pre-battle checks starting with his revolver. He took the bullets out of the gun and spun the barrel while blowing through the holes. As he went about his business he realised he was as terrified as his own men. However, a more sickening feeling was building within him. As he thought about his speech he wondered if it was little more than an echo of the jingoistic demagoguery uttered by the aging political powers that had initiated and prolonged the war. Surely a sane man would tell the troops to lay down their arms and walk home to England, to their homes and families, rather than walk up a hill in the pitch black firing on an invisible enemy armed with machine guns. He thought about Ralph. He wondered how he might have reacted to his name and music being used to help achieve military aims; he certainly knew what Ralph would have thought about the religious angle of his speech. With a host of conflicting thoughts competing for supremacy in his mind, he completed his checks, then rested his head on his peak cap and tried to get some sleep.

George circulated the group and checked that each soldier was prepared for the attack. As he did so he realised that men deal with fear in many different ways. Some, like Millar, turn to stone and stare vacantly into the distance as though hypnotised. Others, like Harford, hide behind excitable and exaggerated humour – much to the annoyance of others. Some, like Sergeant Heywood, a handsome man in his late twenties, with rugged defined features, become silent, reflective and introspective. He had spent his last night not sleeping but composing a sonnet for his wife. Johnson appeared to be well adjusted and confident but was still prone to vomiting at the side of the road. As for George, he refused to acknowledge his feelings. They were all there; fear, anger, terror, homesickness and a knotting apprehension which tied his insides up, but to recognise such feelings or, worse still, be at their mercy would undermine his authority. He was in charge and so had to remain in control.

As the soldiers made their way quietly along the Albert-Bapaume Road, the night sky was illuminated by a larger-than-usual full moon and a host of stars dusting the evening with tiny particles of light. George was reminded of a dear uncle who had once bought him a telescope so that he could look at the stars and the moon which he did on many a summer night. He loved to see the craters on the moon and even saw a shooting star on one happy occasion. But as the angelic light shone down on the fearful men making them increasingly conspicuous, he would have given anything to have pulled them all out of the sky. He feared that it would only be a matter of time before the lunar rays shone on them as they approached the German held village and their cover was blown. But that was not the only reason George wished for darkness. The town was in ruins. The villagers and the French army had been unable to halt the German army's advance, and as such the road to Pozières was strewn with the putrid corpses of villagers and army personnel alike. Shafts of light would highlight the decaying flesh and bones of those who had gone before him and chilled him to the bone. The once beautifully quaint buildings which once stood along the roadside were now scattered over a large area, as though a child had knocked their blocks down in a tantrum. Family possessions were dotted along the road side and amongst the rubble, a poignant reminder of happier times. Children's toys, sepia pictures of beloved parents and, much to the sadness of George, a fine violin were all left to decay with their owners. The trees which would ordinarily be blossoming in bursts of colour and light were little more than scorched remains reaching with jagged limbs up to the sky.

As the road rose to the German vantage point George, alongside Captain Burnham, spotted two German soldiers aimlessly wandering in front of a wall of sandbags. George and Burnham gesticulated to the soldiers to get down and take cover. George, hiding behind a section of wall with a window frame, took aim and waited for his order to fire. The anticipation grew as the company laid themselves down and waited. As George lined up his sights as best he could in the darkness, he could hear the heavy breathing of Millar. He signalled to Johnson next to him to silence Millar which he did by placing his hand over his mouth.

'When you are ready,' whispered Burnham.

George moved his Lee-Enfield as steadily as he could, from left to right, until the German strayed into his sights. With a dry swallow and a short prayer he pulled the trigger. The wandering soldier was stopped in his tracks and George watched as he fell to the floor like a rag doll.

The group remained as still as they could, hoping that the Germans were unsure from which direction the bullet had come. Burnham, peering through binoculars, could see that the other German soldier had fled behind the sand bags into the safety of the compound. No easy follow-up shot would be possible now. The German's would be looking in all directions, making the most of their raised vantage point. On the other side of the road, Johnson had taken up a position behind a fireplace standing undamaged in the rubble of another house. Burnham signed to him to supply covering fire while the rest of the troops found cover on either side of the road. As he let fire the men duly took up positions in the devastated houses before return fire commenced with vigour. Each gun shot on one side of the road was followed by an advance forward by a gunner on the other side. The incessant fire from the Germans was enough to slow the advance down but George and his men made steady gains a foot or so at a time.

George shouted to Burnham, now held up behind a ruined coal bunker on the other side of the road, 'Captain, we need to speed things up before Gerry brings out the big guns.'

Captain Burnham nodded in agreement just as a bullet struck the side of the bunker spraying him with dust. 'Ok lads let's get moving before the big bangs come. On my mark, the company will advance!'

'Listen to the music boys!' George shouted. 'Listen to the music!'

'One!' Burnham screamed, as he watched one of his men fall from behind a large oak beam. 'Two!'

George inhaled deep and waited as another bullet struck the ground in front of him.

'THREE!'

The company moved out firing almost without aim, straight at the German compound. As George ran forward he could feel the blood pumping and thumping in his head, his breaths deeper but shorter and the sweat running from his brow dripped into his eyes and made them sting. He quickly wiped them so that he could see his way forward before losing his feet and tumbling into a shell hole in the road. He tried to pick himself up but as he did so felt his hand ooze into something cold, wet and pungent. He focused his sweat-soaked eyes and saw that he had fallen into a mass grave and had unknowingly sunk his hand deep into the acrid and decaying stomach of a French soldier. He screamed in repulsion and could feel the vile taste of vomit on his own tongue. He wretched but nothing came. He could feel the crawling of parasitic invertebrates on his hand but dare not look at them. He wiped his hand clean on his uniform, picked up his weapon and made his way out of the hole and onward up the road.

Ten yards further forward Millar had made good progress toward the Germans and was taking up intelligent positions of cover before letting loose his return fire. Considering that Millar could hardly move a few hours earlier, George was amazed at the soldier's bravery. As George took up another position of cover five yards further ahead he watched Millar take out a German gunner with a clean shot to the face. George returned fire with his pistol and as he did so he could see German soldiers heading out on either flank to meet the company in man to man battle.

Most of the approaching soldiers were duly dispatched by the bullets from English rifles and pistols while George,

Burnham and the rest of the men made their way forward. Making further inroads George saw Johnson trip in the road and lose his rifle as an enemy soldier closed in on him. Before the corporal could recover his weapon or draw his pistol from its holster, a bayonet slipped through his torso. The German twisted the blade before withdrawing it and returning it deep into Johnson's throat just below his chin. George took aim with his pistol and shot the German clean in the heart and watched him fall on Johnson's body.

George then made his way forward another five yards and fired at another enemy soldier, wounding him in the leg and then saw Harford follow up and shoot the soldier in the back of the head. Harford stood up and looked back at George proudly.

'Get down Harford…' yelled George.

But before the words had even reached the Private a sniper's bullet went straight into his chest and he fell hard. George could see that Harford was still alive and quickly made his way to him, unloading a whole chamber of cover fire from his pistol along the way. He slumped his body along side Harford who was screaming in agony. The blood was seeping from beneath his right collarbone. George pulled his medical kit out from his side, took out a bandage and crumpled it up and applied pressure to the wound, much to Harford's discomfort.

'Emerson! Get over here,' ordered George.

The lanky soldier whose height did nothing to make him less conspicuous, fired off a chamber from his pistol as he made his way up the road to where George and Harford were held up.

'Emerson, help me get him out of here before they take another pop at us.' The sound of bullets thudding into the ground around them seemed to draw closer. 'You get one arm, I'll get the other. Make for the church ruin over there.'

'Yes, Sir.'

Harford wailed as George and Emerson dragged him over the bricks and rubble to a standing wall, complete with a shattered stain-glass window, at the side of the road. Beyond the wall George removed the first aid kit from Harford's side and used another bandage to soak up the escaping blood.

'Here,' said George to an out-of-breath Emerson, 'you take over.'

'But we don't have enough bandages.'

George took off his jacket quickly and rolled it into a ball and placed it over Harford's wound. He pushed down hard on the wound and the soldier screamed in pain. He took Emerson's hands and placed them on the jacket.

'Here, keep the pressure on the wound. Give him lots of water and stay with him, no matter what. Do you understand?'

Emerson swallowed, 'Yes, Sir.'

George looked at the shaking Harford and smiled at him as the moonlight kissed his face. 'Told you you'd be fine. You've got a Blighty wound, old boy.'

George picked up his rifle and pistol and made his way back to the road. As he took up a firing position beyond a pile of rubble he saw Millar shoot an oncoming enemy soldier in the leg. He could see the soldier's leg pop open and spray blood into the night air and then watched him fall. Millar followed up with his bayonet and, letting out a piercing cry, skewered the soldier in the heart with all his strength. He took out his blade, paused for a second and stabbed him again and again with increasing ferocity, before falling to his knees and placing his head and hands on the German's body and breaking out into an uncontrollable and hysterical cry.

'I'm sorry! I'm sorry!' he wailed. 'Forgive me!'

Millar rolled off the body and began to dig into the earth and rubble with his hands. When he had dug a modest hole, he curled himself into a ball rested in it. George sprinted as fast as he could over to him.

'Millar!' he said. 'It's okay. I'm here.'

'I want my Mum, Sir,' he cried. 'I just want my Mum.'

'I know boy,' he cradled him in his arms for a moment. 'I know, but we're nearly there. Look, there are fewer German's coming now, which means the Anzacs have started their manoeuvres. Come on, son! On your feet!'

George continued his advance up the road until he, Millar, Burnham, Boon, Heywood and Thomas were within forty yards of the German compound. As each of them took cover where they could, Burnham gave the order to bomb and follow. After another count of three the soldiers removed the pin from their Mills Bombs and sent them hurtling toward the stars and into the German defences. Before the German's could throw their grenade sticks, there were six ear-splitting explosions. No sooner had the mud, sand and other debris settled, the company charged over the sandbags of the German compound and cleared the remaining gunners. Much to George's surprise there hardly any enemy soldiers left in the compound. As he checked for survivors, of which there were none, he saw to the other side of the road, through a hole in the sandbags and could see the last remaining Germans engaged in battle with the Anzacs.

Their work, for now, was done. George looked back down the road from where he had come and saw it was littered with bodies. Some of his finest men had fallen, some were writhing on the ground. He sent Boon, Heywood and Thomas back to retrieve them for treatment in the clearing station as soon as the ambulance corps arrived. George ran his hands through his hair, sat on an open sandbag and stared into the fixed and dilated pupils of a German soldier as the light from the moon shone kindly on his face. He leaned forward and carefully lowered the soldiers eyelids then sat back down and looked away from the ugliness on the ground to the beauty in the night sky.

Sleep in Ecoivres was uncomfortable. Harry and Ralph rested together in the back of the ambulance and listened to the distant rumbles of artillery fire. Occasionally they could see the sky illuminate with alabaster-white hues before returning to darkness, followed a few seconds later by the accompanying bang. However, after weeks of aiding the wounded and retrieving the dead in hell they were beginning to get used to the discomfort. The same moonlight that shone on George in Pozières now crept through the tiny holes in the canvas which covered the roof of the ambulance. Ralph lay on his back and rested his hands, the fingers laced together on his chest and called to Harry. When no response came Ralph assumed that Harry had finally entered his slumber and sighed. He could not sleep. It was impossible. Beyond the myriad of thoughts which confused and tangled his mind into a web of contradictions, he heard the echo of the bugle call which he had first heard in England. The imperfection of the misplayed motif grated on him and there was no way to put it right.

He wondered how Adeline was coping with her illness and yearned for her to the point that he could feel tears building in the corners of his eyes. He wondered what the future might hold for him as a composer – would the ideas and the inspiration return or was he condemned to a lifetime of mediocrity? He wondered then what the future might hold for him as a protagonist in the war. Finally, he wondered where his friend might be and if he was safe. As the melody and thoughts battled for control of his mind, Ralph sighed once more turned over on his side and closed his eyes.

As the morning sun staggered above the horizon and shone above the desolation of Pozières, George marvelled at its loveliness and majesty. Yet he mourned the irony that only the perfect beauty of the morning sun could properly illuminate the carnage of the night before. He made his way through the rubble and corpses which scattered the main road and only then could grasp the enormity of what had happened. He passed the bloodied heads and bodies of men who had fought simply because they had been told to. Did they really believe? George had his doubts. He stood at the feet of the German whom he had shot dead to initiate the attack. He took no pride in what he had done. The shot was clean to the temple, he would have felt nothing, but this was scant consolation to him. He couldn't negate the simple truth that he had killed a man, a son, perhaps a father, and he felt sick. He thought of Ralph's words back in Hunstanton, how he spoke of "blind faith" and "jingoism" and wondered if, as the slaughter continued, the more his contentions became valid and commanded respect.

George was proud of his men; the way they fought through their fear, the way they fought the voices inside their heads telling that they were about to commit suicide and, simply, the way they fought. However, the loss of Johnson was hard to bare and he couldn't escape the thought that he had lied to him. He told the men that they would get out of their hell, but Johnson's assassin had made a liar out of him. The guilt was too much to take at that moment. George had killed a number of Germans that night and placed his hands in the acrid corpse of a French fighter but there only appeared to be Johnson's blood on his hands.

As Johnson's commanding officer he volunteered to write to the corporal's family informing him of his death. How, George wondered, does one write that kind of letter? Later that night he tore a page out of his note, on the back of which were a number of musical sketches in faded pencil, and sat down to write. Bizarrely, George found himself worrying about his spelling and punctuation; was there a 't' in conscientious and was it 'i' before 'e' or the other way around. He wrote slowly so as to offer Johnson's parent's his finest handwriting, although he knew, completely, that such attention to presentation would, in no way, soften the blow of his death. But that was all he could offer them. He also found an iota of solace in praising Johnson's courage and dedication. He told them of his larger-than-life character and how he kept the morale of the group high by telling irreverent jokes. Finally, he reviewed the letter and considered what to tell his parents about the nature of their son's death. Should he tell them the truth; that Johnson's last few seconds consisted of a feeling of pure terror and fear, followed by the agony and horror of seeing deep into the eyes of another human being as he sunk a twelve inch blade into his stomach? He concluded that it would be easier on Johnson's family to believe that their beloved had died instantly with a sniper's shot, clean through the head. It was a lie, he thought, but one more wouldn't make any difference.

# CHAPTER TEN

The ambulance jolted and bucked like an angry stallion as it negotiated its way along the pitted road from Ecoivres to the field hospital some ten miles away from the line. The clearing station was completely full and all injuries were sent straight to the field hospital. Lying on a stretcher on one side of the ambulance young private Cowan struggled to remain calm. The shrapnel implanted in his groin caused him to yawp with every movement of the vehicle, and the urine which every-so-often would seep into the wound did nothing to alleviate the pain. Harry did his best to keep the pressure on the wound, pushing down hard with both hands. Cowan was sweating profusely and Ralph mopped his brow with a towel as the ambulance swayed from side to side, up and down, and all uncomfortable points in between.

At the field hospital Cowan was unloaded without ceremony and guided straight to the treatment room. The doctors and nurses helped carry the patient on to the relative comfort of an army hospital bed and began to administer a mix of chloroform and ether to alleviate the pain. That signalled the end of a shift for Harry and Ralph.

'He should be alright now, mate,' Harry assured a concerned looking Ralph as they headed outside to get a breath of fresh air.

'He shouldn't even be here.'

'Well that's the risk you take when you're a soldier.'

'That's not what I mean.' Ralph tightened his lips, 'I'm sick of treating children. I'm tired of bringing out the bodies of boys who shouldn't even be here.'

'Well there's not much we can do about it.'

'We shouldn't have to do anything about it, they shouldn't be here. He was seventeen. And who cares?'

'People care.'

'Who? The old swines in the conservative club, reading the casualty lists over a nice glass of port? What about Haig? Do you think he cares?'

'No and perhaps he shouldn't.'
Ralph looked incredulously at Harry,' What on earth do you mean?'

'Well… he's got a job to do. He's got a war to win. In war people die. Do you want him blubbing at the casualty list or do you want him to create battle plans? There's nothing he can do about the dead.'

'Since when did you become Haig's greatest admirer?'
'Come on mate, there's no need for that,' said Harry trying to calm the situation with chirpiness. 'All I'm saying is that it's easy to criticise, but what would you do if you were in charge?'

'Well, I certainly wouldn't send these boys out into no man's land and order them to *walk* to the German's.' Harry shrugged his shoulders. 'I'm sorry old boy. I know it's only been a few weeks but I can see what's happening here.'

'And what's that?' asked Harry

'We have a whole generation – supposedly the older and the wiser – sending the *next* generation out to their death to save them. There's has to be a better way.'

'Well, if you can work out something that they haven't thought about, I'm sure they'd like to hear from you. With your position you could speak out against the war and people would listen.'

'I don't want to speak out,' said Ralph.

'Why not?'

'I'll not do anything publicly that will undermine the army. What good will that do for the troops?'

'Well, you can't have it both ways, Ralph mate.'

Harry wandered off, leaving Ralph standing outside the makeshift hospital – a small church in the middle of the countryside. He looked around and couldn't escape the irony of being in a hospital which was literally surrounded by death in the form of unkempt gravestones and derelict monuments to the deceased. Ralph, despite holding agnostic views, had always liked churches. He marvelled at their sense of splendour and was amazed that man could erect buildings so grandiose in the name of God, that their faith in the unseen and the unheard was so unwavering and unquestioning that they would literally spend years of their lives creating them. When in a churchyard Ralph always found himself liable to question his own mortality and existential thoughts were never far away. He would find himself asking what Socrates might have called the big questions; who are we? Where are we? Why are we here? All of those questions seemed to assume more poignancy and profundity in the time of war.

The summer heat had become sticky and oppressive. It seemed to smother Ralph. He couldn't escape it. The air was close and as he sat on an overgrown, rectangular tombstone supported in each corner by urn-shaped stilts, he took in a long, deep breath. He reached into his pocket and found the picture of George looking, he thought, more innocent than he could ever be again. He remembered the quaint little melody that George wrote in the sand at Hunstanton and wondered if he would ever write anything as pure and untainted again. George's music had always been a source of great solace for Ralph. Although much younger than him, George had a talent for melody. Ralph always found melodies hard to come by, harmonies and rhythms came naturally, but he had to toil relentlessly for tunes. George's tunes always seemed like a celebration; as if he were blissfully unaware that music could be angry or sad. In short George's music was a reflection of all that was good, all that was beautiful, innocent and pure. Now that the war had cast a ubiquitous shadow over the lives of all of his composer friends – Geoffrey, Reggie, George and even Gustav – he wondered what might happen to those tunes. Would they ring with national pride on the war's conclusion or would dissonance mark the music like a scar on the Mona Lisa? What would happen to the melodies? Would they sound at all or would the war take those who would bring new music to the world? Where would all that beauty go? Could it ever be replaced? Once again Ralph tried to marshal his wandering thoughts as best he could, but each thought introduced another idea and a counter idea, until a complex web of opinions, judgments, feelings and emotions became entangled in his brain. Wearily, he reclined and rested his head on the tombstone. As he did so he felt the first weighty drops of summer rain fall upon his face. The rain began to fall more heavily but he felt no compulsion to retire inside the hospital. Instead he took off his coat and shirt until his bare chest stared up into the sky. He let the rain fall on him and wash him clean; clean of the mud and blood, and clean of his thoughts; if only for a short while.

An hour or so passed. The precipitation abated, soon to pass completely and the humid summer air had begun to dry Ralph as he lay on the tomb, yet his hair was still drenched in rain and sweat. As he rested, finally thinking of nothing in particular, Harry peered over him and dropped a towel on his chest.

'Here, you'll need this, you old sod.'
Ralph sat up and placed the towel over his shoulders. 'Thank you.'

'I'm sorry,' said Harry.

'No, I'm the one who should apologise,' Ralph replied with a sigh. 'You were right I can't have it both ways. I think I've been searching for the perfect solution to an imperfect war. It's just… I see those boys come in to the hospital and I think what's going to happen in the future.'

'I know mate.'

'How do you remain sane in a place like this?'

'Who says I'm sane?' Harry crossed his eyes and banged his temple as if to roll them back into position. Ralph chuckled. 'Anyway, you're talking to a man who nearly killed one of his own. Or had you forgotten about that?'

'But there seems to be so much madness now that sanity is out of the ordinary. Where is the sanity in *walking* those boys toward the machine guns? Where is the sanity in killing a young man you have never met, plunging a bayonet into his body, seeing the blood come gurgling up out of his mouth, calling out for his mother… because somebody else you have never met tells you to? I wonder if the boys in the German trenches ask these questions at all. I mean do any of the boys really know what they're fighting for?'

'I doubt it.'

'But you're right we can't have it both ways. But, you know, I think it is the contradictions that perpetuate my anger. I want to win the war, but I don't want to see any more death; it can't be done. I want to be home with Adeline but don't want to leave my responsibilities here; I can't have both.'

'You know your problem, Ralph?' asked Harry putting his arm around him. 'You think too much!'

Harry picked up the towel and playfully dropped it on Ralph's head.

'Now dry yourself off, you daft old git, before you catch a cold. I'll see if I can find us a cuppa.'

The 23rd Division of the Durham Light Infantry were back

in the trenches at Somme following their exploits at Pozières. Much to George's anger his men were denied a period of leave following the battle, but he continued to do what he could to keep up morale. The daily routine of uniform and equipment inspections continued, and this even allowed George a few moments to indulge in some composition.

The day began like any other, with George boiling water for the men's early morning tea. He poured the boiling water then placed a spoonful of powdered milk into a dozen or so cups, shared a teabag between three and disseminated them around the company. Then, after carrying out his paternal service, he sat down with his own mug of colourless tea. As he took his first sip he heard a timid but well-spoken voice.

'Uh, hello, Sir,' his voice quivered, 'is this 23rd Division.'

'Yes.'

'Ah, well at least I have the right place. I've been sent here by...' he looked confused, '...well I suppose the recruiting office, really.'

'Yes,' George said shaking the boy's hand. 'So you must be Humbert?'

'Yes, Sir. Edward Humbert.'

George had always done his best not to let first impressions turn into judgments, but in Humbert's case it was difficult. The first thing he noticed about Humbert was his femininity. George had no qualms with the boys supposed sexuality but he did wonder how some of the others might react to him. Humbert was also very slight and as he stood before his new superior, he seemed to struggle to hold his rifle and the rest of his army issue. His balance shifted from one side to the other and he looked far from comfortable. His pale smooth face with the first signs of stubble, sky-blue eyes and lips so red that he appeared to be wearing lipstick, only served to make him stand out from the battle-worn soldiers in the company.

'Well, Humbert, it's nice to have you here, let me

introduce you to the chaps.'

George duly took the boy down the line to meet the men who offered polite, yet less-than-warm, greetings. As they did so, Humbert jumped and then cowered at every explosion, while the other soldiers were almost indifferent to the din.

'It's just noise,' said Millar as he made the boy's acquaintance. 'You get used to it after a while.'

'Really?'

'Yeah, you'll be alright.'

The sentiment echoed in George's mind and for a moment he thought of the same promise he gave to Johnson. George and Humbert carried on down the trench until they came to the communication dugout. The entrance to the dugout consisted of three large beams of oak in the trench wall and a make-shift room consisting of a desk, complete with telephone and morse telegraph, and a bed which had been crudely put together using some ammunition boxes and some blankets. George took a seat at the desk while Humbert sat down on the bed, still gripping his rifle tightly.

'So,' said George merrily, 'where are you from?

'Uhm, well I'm originally from London, but my father owns a factory in Derbyshire so we've lived there for the last ten years or so.'

'Oh,' said George suspiciously, 'so you would have been what, eight years old.'

'No I think I was about seven when we…' he stopped in his tracks having realised the trap he was falling into. '…I mean, no, I think I was eight.'

'Humbert?' George raised his eyebrows like and expectant teacher waiting for the attention of a disruptive pupil.

'Sir?'

'The truth!"

The boy sighed in resignation. 'I'm seventeen.'

'I thought so.'

'But I'll be eighteen soon.'

'Really?' said an unimpressed George.

'Yes, in about eight months.'

'That's not what I would consider soon. What the hell are you doing here?'

'What does it matter? I'm here now.'

'It matters a great deal.'

'The army's not going to bother now is it? I'm not the only under-age soldier.'

'That's not the bloody point!' snapped George. 'It matters to me.'

George stood up and rubbed his head in frustration. The time for friendliness had now been and gone. Now straight talking was in order.

'Last week I watched one of my men die. I saw him…' George thought for a moment and decided to spare Humbert the gory details. 'I do not intend to watch a child die.'

'But I'm not a child, Sir.'

'In the eyes of the law you are.' George shouted. 'This is serious. I have men here who are still children when it comes to facing the enemy.'

'I'm sorry, Sir,' cowered Humbert. 'I just thought that…'

'…That what? That you might be able to get a little bit of glory? Because there's nothing glorious here. You didn't think it through at all.'

'I'm not useless.'

'No, I'm sure you're not. Gerry likes to have someone young to aim at.'

'I've had training.'

'Training is one thing, reality is another. I'm sure you dealt with those sack full of straw more than ably but it's another thing to stick it to a Bosch.' George stood up and towered over Humbert. 'You wait here.'

'What are you going to do?'

'I'm going to try and get you out of here, and now.'

'But I can fight.'

'No, you can't.'

'DON'T TELL ME I CAN'T!' screamed Humbert, with fire in his eyes.

George was taken aback. There was a real anger and fear in Humbert's face. It almost seemed that he was more afraid of going home than being blown to pieces in battle. George paused for a while as the boy calmed.

'You mustn't speak to your commanding officer in that tone.' George placed his head in his hands and puffed out his cheeks. 'Just get out!'

Humbert stood up and left the dugout, before cautiously turning around outside. 'Please, sir…'

'I said get out!'

George, still with his head in his hands, tugged at his hair to relieve the tension inside. He took a seat on the bed and sighed. With the roar of the distant guns pounding in his head he closed his eyes and within a short while slumber took him elsewhere.

George found himself on the beach once again. It was like Hunstanton but there were strange cars driving up and down the beach. The sun was shining and the day seemed happy and serene. As George paddled along the shore he felt a tugging at his trouser leg. He looked down and a little boy with flaxen hair was holding out a conch shell.

'Look what I found George,' he said.

'Oh! Isn't that lovely?'

'You can keep it if you like.'

'That's very kind of you, young man.'

The boy smiled and carried on along the shore. Another car pulled up along side him on the beach and a host of children came out of them playing merrily; splashing and thrashing the shallows to a foam. He looked behind him and dozens of other cars were driving past and unloading hundreds of young boys and girls. Some children made sandcastles, others dug huge holes in the sand and began to fill them with water. Skinny, pale toddlers ran around naked while young boys in swimming trunks began a game of cricket, and young girls skipped rope or played on the hopscotch grid scratched into the wet sand. Another young child came up alongside George and showed him another conch shell.

'Look inside this one, George.' The little boy extended his arm and offered him the shell.

George held the shell in his hand and saw a hermit crab poking out his claws and antennae. As he went to touch the crab it peered out of his home and heard a loud explosion. The crustacean retreated quickly into its shell. George winced. The next thing he saw was a desolate beach. Nothing but the sound of the wind howling along the shore. There was no sign of the children but as he looked down at his feet he found hundreds of conch shells piled high around him. Curiously he bent down and picked one up and tipped it on its opening. As it tilted slowly brilliant red blood began to trickle out of the shell hole. A huge explosion nearby startled him from his dream. He sat bolt upright, breathing heavily with sweat running down his face. He lifted his legs up in front of him and placed his head between his knees. He felt salty perspiration run behind his ears, along his cheeks and into his mouth. As the might of the German army did its best to shower the trench with all it could muster, George wept silently.

That night the dream would not leave George's mind. He could not sleep. Every time he lowered his eyes he saw the blood running from the conch shell and any brief respite from the sound of artillery fire was punctuated with the echoes of his own screams of madness. He wondered what Ralph might have made of his dream. Ralph had spent some time in Paris studying orchestration under Maurice Ravel, one of the most noted impressionist composers. On his return he had told George about the extent to which the Impressionists were influenced by dream states. He also told him about the writings of Sigmund Freud. George had come to understand that, if

Freudian theory were applied, dreams were a form of wish-fulfillment. On the face of it this would seem absurd if applied to George's dream. He put his amateur Freudian psychotherapy into practice. First, the beach was a place that he associated with happiness. Many of the most joyous occasions in his life had taken place next to the sea, be it the holidays to Scarborough that he spent with his family or the summer days walking along the shore at Hunstanton, singing folk songs with Ralph. Perhaps, he thought, this was the extent of the concept of wish-fulfillment. While in the trenches he would often think of the Norfolk shoreline, with its long extended sandy beaches and dunes peppered with tufts of long grass. But what of the children? The obvious explanation would be to associate them with the young soldiers in his trench – some of them children themselves. However, George couldn't escape the idea that the children were simply a symbol of innocence; but whose? The war had taken the innocence of many a man. As much as even the most dedicated soldier might try, the act of killing another human being pulls him further away from his own humanity. Indeed, every killing that George made on the battlefield, every one of his own that he saw cut to shreds by maschinengewehr or blown to pieces by shell-fire, every life that was taken pushed George one step further from his childhood, his dreams, his hopes and yet further away from any thoughts of the future. Miles from home, miles from his past and miles from his future, George had considered the possibility that his life would henceforth be conducted in the present.

But, what of the conch shells? Could it be that they represented a hiding place, somewhere to escape to, just as the hermit crab had retreated at the sight of George's hand. Could it be that it represented the concept of home. He had tried to keep memories of his home alive during his time in France. In his mind he would often walk up the steep hills in Warfdale in Yorkshire near his childhood home, he would try to recall all the nuances of the area – the sound of bleating lambs, the smell of pure fresh mountain air and the feel of the gravel paths beneath his feet.

Finally, he turned his attention to the blood. Whose blood was it? He considered that it could be the blood of the young, who had so swiftly disappeared from the beach. However, he also entertained the notion that the blood was his own and this filled his bones with fear. Holding on to hope and faith was getting harder day by day.

# CHAPTER ELEVEN

The early morning sunbeams shone life onto the lifeless faces in the recovery ward at the field hospital. Ralph had risen early that morning so that he could check on some of the wounded he had brought in. At first glance the rows of neatly folded beds seemed like the gravestones in the cemetery outside, neat and fixed. The boys and men within the white army sheets seemed motionless. He walked the length of the ward and watched the men resting. Some had lost limbs, others had lost their mind. Nurses wandered through the ward like beautiful ghosts as though the things they had seen had numbed their emotions. Their faces were indifferent, not that they did not care, but it was as though they had been forced to block out their feelings in order to cope with the horrors they saw each and every day. He saw a young man adorned with beautiful red hair sat up on the bed with his knees raised up to his chin and his arms wrapped tightly around his shins. His brilliant blue eyes glistened as they stared vacantly into the distance, seemingly unable to concentrate on anything in particular. His hunched body seemed to find no solace in embracing itself, it trembled and shuddered constantly. His face was pale, the anaemic complexion dotted with child-like freckles. Ralph felt a strange compulsion to talk to the boy, a combination of pity, compassion and curiosity. Nervousness delayed him and he struggled to think of what to say. He looked at the boy's chart on the end of the bed. It seemed as good a starting point for a conversation as any.

'Callum Strachan, hey?' The boy looked at Ralph without moving any part of his slender body. 'So, how are you?'

As soon as the words passed his lips he cursed himself inside, what a stupid question, he thought. The boy said nothing.

'I don't remember bringing you in,' said Ralph, 'you must have come in with one of the other ambulances.'

Still Strachan said nothing, still he remained motionless aside from his worsening shakes. Ralph persevered. This time he decided that he would do the talking as Strachan was clearly saying nothing.

'It's a nice setting here, isn't it?' He looked around the church masquerading as a hospital and took in the splendour of the architecture. 'I'm not a believer, but that doesn't mean I don't appreciate this. And I'm open to the fact that I might be wrong.'

Ralph moved forward and sat on the end of Strachan's bed. The patient, again without moving, watched him all the way. Ralph could see that the boy was frightened and so decided to keep the conversation light.

'I uh… I'm a composer. A musician. I play the viola… badly. I also teach. I'm not a great teacher though. I don't really have the patience.' An awkward silence ensued. 'I live in London, but I've got a place in Norfolk too. It's lovely. I've got a wife. Her name is Adeline. She's very pretty. Too pretty for me. She plays the cello… She's very good. But she struggles with her health. She has rheumatoid Arthritis so she finds it hard, you know, with the bowing and the finger patterns. I remember when the doctor told us. It was a bit of a bombshell really and…'

Before Ralph could finish his sentence Strachan leapt

off his bed and screamed hysterically as if possessed. The sound of his screams cut through Ralph and terrified him like an inescapable nightmare. Strachan scrambled under the bed and placed his hands on his head. He curled up once again in the foetus position as tight as he could, his knuckles white and clenched rigidly. As the nurses came running to attend to him he watched a pool of urine appear from underneath Strachan and trickle out from beneath the bed. The potent smell made Ralph wretch. He panicked. He could feel the hairs on the back of his neck stand firmly on end, he struggled to catch his breath, he felt an unwelcome heat surge through his body and in fear, terror and humiliation he ran out of the ward and into the church gardens. He ran as though running in a nightmare, where the feet don't seem to touch the ground. As he sprinted manically into the early morning light he turned back and watched more nurses running into the church. He still couldn't catch his breath and soon he could feel sweat running down his face and creeping down the back of his neck. He turned once again and ran straight into the arms of Harry.

'It's alright, Ralph,' he said holding on to his friend tightly. 'It's alright! It's alright.'

But Ralph hardly seemed to recognise Harry. His breathing continued to labour and now the shivers which afflicted Strachan now seemed to take hold of Ralph. Harry pulled Ralph closer still and embraced him like a mother holding a crying child.

'It's alright, Ralph. I'm here.'

It took an hour or so for Ralph to calm completely and come to terms with what he had witnessed. Harry informed him that Strachan had been brought in a few weeks earlier and had what the doctors were calling neurasthenia, others simply called it shell shock. According to Harry, Strachan had been in a trench near Verdun when the communication line where he was stationed came under heavy artillery fire. He was trapped beneath dozens of sandbags which had caved in on him as the trench wall collapsed. He watched the shelling continue around him for the next hour before a massive explosion, where upon a hand landed on the sandbags right before him. The doctors at the hospital had established that upon even the most casual utterance of the word "bomb" something would trigger in his mind and he would dash for cover under his bed, screaming out in terror. Ralph was consumed with guilt. His seemingly innocuous and trivial conversation had precipitated a moment of awfulness so intense that he had inadvertently taken Strachan back to the very moment where his mind was taken.

'You okay now, mate?'

'Yes, thank you Harry.' Ralph inhaled deeply. 'I don't know what came over me. I don't know what happened.'

'It was a shock for you.'

'Yes, but I've seen far worse than that in the field. I've seen dead people. I've seen all of that… stuff.'

'I know, mate,' said Harry sympathetically. 'But it's not about the broken bones or the shrapnel wounds is it? I mean, you can see them. But then there are the broken minds. You can't see them. You can't see how bad the wound is inside. You don't know how deep it goes. You can't see if it has infected the mind… until something snaps. Then you see the extent of the wound. And that's far more frightening than the physical wounds.'

'The poor boy.' Ralph massaged the tear-ducts in his eyes and rubbed the bridge of his nose. 'I just wanted to help.'

'He'll be okay,' said Harry. 'They're sending him to Edinburgh soon. He's going to that Craiglockhart place. You know? Where they treat the shell-shockers?'

Ralph mopped the sweat away from his forehead and into the recession of his hairline.

'What can I do, Harry?' His cockney friend shrugged his shoulders. 'I can't just leave them here with their nightmares.'

'I don't know mate. I don't know.'

The gunfire had been heavy all morning. Shelling along the line was constant. Humbert grasped his rifle until the bones came close to busting out of the skin around his knuckles. His breathing was erratic and he wept like a child. He was detailed to fire on the enemy positions opposite but could barely raise his head to within a foot of the trench top, let alone look over, take aim and shoot. His knees seemed to struggle to take the weight of his meagre body under the strain of fear and heavy equipment. With his rifle pointing upward, leant against the sandbags he rested his forehead on the barrel of his weapon and tried to gather his composure. He swallowed hard and took a deep breath then slowly raised his body until he could see into no-man's land. He could see no sign of the German gunners but, nevertheless, pulled his gun around and fired indiscriminately into the distance before sliding back down the wall.

George came down the line of the trench, striding purposefully and tall, to check on his men's progress.

'How are we getting on, gentlemen?'

The men gave their individual reports; how many rounds they had fired, how many they had left and how many, if any, kills they had made. He could see that Humbert would have none of this information.

'You okay, Humbert?' he asked.

Humbert tried to exhibit some semblance of maturity but George could see right through the pretence. 'Yes, Lieutenant.'

'Keep at it then.'

A few feet away three gunners had their rifles inserted into long pipes which ran through the trench wall and pointed at the German defences. This enabled the British snipers to take aim at the enemy from the relative safety of the trench wall. With monotonous regularity they would shoot round after round down the pipes and, occasionally into the tender bodies of the young Hun opposite.

The gunner nearest Humbert was a well-built heroic figure

## The Pastoral

with a cigarette pointing out of the corner of his mouth, even while shooting. Humbert waited for a lull in the firing and then approached the sniper.

'Can I look through there?'

The sniper looked at the slender boy. 'What's your name?'

'Humbert.'

'Humbert, hey?' said the confident soldier. 'Well, I don't see why not.'

'Thank you, Mister...?'

'Hatfield.' He dragged nonchalantly on his cigarette. '*Sergeant* Hatfield. None of this Mister business, hey mate? You're in the army now.'

'Yes, Sergeant.'

Humbert looked down the piping and could see the twisting lines of barbed wire and, just beyond them, the German trenches. He could see corpses lying rigid in the mud and shell holes scattered around the slight incline of no-man's land.

'Oh my god!' said Humbert.

'Lovely, isn't it?' said Hatfield sarcastically.

'Have you killed many?'

'Enough to keep me here all bloody day.' Hatfield resumed his position looking down the pipe, his rifle inserted inside and resting perfectly still. He fired a shot.

'Did you hit them?' asked Humbert innocently.

'Not this time. But there's always…'

Before Hatfield could finish his sentence a pinpoint shot from a German sniper found its way, with deadly purpose, down the small opening of the pipe and with a quiet thud straight into Hatfield's eye. The bullet was true and went through Hatfield's skull and caused a small precipitation of blood to scatter on to Humbert's face. The sergeant's limp and instantly-lifeless body collapsed to the floor, the residue of the bullet rose from his disfigured face, while Humbert stood motionless staring at the body. There was a hive of morbid activity as Hatfield's friends held his body and cried out manically. Some picked up his body and took it away down the trench line, while a young private took a bucket of water and a rag and cleaned Hatfield's blood from off the trench wall. Still, Humbert stood motionless and silent. For a moment, all he could hear was the blood pumping around his ears, everything appeared to take place in slow-motion and all he could feel was the rise and fall of his chest as he breathed in and out. He was unaware of the incessant and ubiquitous shelling, it was as though he was on the stage of a terrible drama and had forgotten his lines. After what seemed like a lifetime he thought he heard the mumbled calling of his name.

'Humbert!' shouted George. He spun him around and forced the boy to look him in the eye. 'Are you okay?'

'I… I uh… He was just… I was just… I was just talking to him. Then…he was…'

'Alright son. It's okay.' George placed a reassuring hand on Humbert's shoulder. 'Go and clean your face. When you've done that go and take a break. I'll speak to you later. Go!'

Humbert took a while to respond, but a comforting pat on shoulder was enough to nudge him back to life. He made his way down the trench line dragging his Lee Enfield along the ground. George watched him all the way.

As night began to fall in the trench George was sat at a desk in the dugout writing some musical sketches in his note book by gas light. He whistled the tune back to himself, looked at it again and made a small correction before humming the revision. He nodded to himself and looked proudly upon his work, when Humbert knocked on the frame of the dugout.

'You wanted to see me, Lieutenant.'

'Yes, come in Humbert.'

'Can I get you a tea?'

'I don't really feel like anything, Sir.'

'Oh, hogwash! Get something warm inside you, boy. It'll do you the world of good.' George poured some hot water onto a teabag which had so far survived two previous attacks of boiling water, then added half a teaspoon of powdered milk. He handed the meagre beverage to Humbert who collected the drink in shaking hands. 'There you are, get that down you.'

'Thank you.'

'Are you okay now?'

Humbert sat down at the desk. 'One minute I was talking to him…'

'I know.'

'It was like it wasn't real. It was as though I wasn't there. I just couldn't move. I didn't know what to do. I mean I've gone through all the training but…'

'But it can never prepare you for seeing the moment.'

'The moment?

'The moment when life stops, when you actually see… death. Because you actually miss a little piece of you dying too. It affects people in different ways. You're stronger than you think though. You're certainly stronger than *I* thought you were.'

'But I froze. I broke down.'

'I've seen men older than you that couldn't handle it as well as you did. I mean you're here, now, talking to me. We're having a cup of tea and having this conversation. Others have seen less than you saw today and are now incapable of saying a word. Some went blind without any injury to their eyes, their brain had simply told them not to see anymore. I know it doesn't feel like it now but you were lucky. You *are* lucky.'

'I was looking down the pipe less than a minute earlier.'

'Well there you are. My point exactly.'

'I feel…guilty.'

George sighed, shook his head and took a long sip of tea. 'Don't. It won't do you any good. It won't bring Hatfield back.'

'But don't you feel guilty when… when it's someone else?

'I did. But then I resolved to postpone my shame until this whole sorry mess is over.'

'What do you mean?'

'Well, I've been lucky so far.' He closed the book on his composition, leaving a stubby pencil inside. 'I've no illusions that I will be lucky tomorrow or the day after.'

'Yes. Quite,' said Humbert slurping his tea and then grimacing.

'I know, it's not great, but it's better than nothing, and you need your strength.' George took another swig. 'I'm sorry I was so short with you the other day.'

'Oh,' Humbert shrugged his shoulders, 'it's okay.'

'No, I was unfair. I just… This is a dreadful place and you should be… somewhere else.' He swallowed the last dregs of tea and placed the metal cup down on the desk with a bang. 'But since you're here…'

'I'm sure you can find some use for me, Sir.'
George wiped away the last few drops of tea from his moustache. 'What do your parents think about your participation in this mess then?'

'I don't really know, Sir.' He paused for a moment. 'I didn't really hang around to find out.'

'I don't understand. They do know you're here, don't they?'

'Yes, they know.'

'And?'

'And my mother is probably missing me.'

'What of your father.'
Humbert sighed and bowed his head. 'He's a different kettle of fish.'

'What do you mean?' George sat back in his chair and listened attentively to Humbert.

'My father is… difficult.'

'In what way?'

Humbert shuffled uncomfortably. 'I have always been something of a disappointment to him.'

'I'm sure that's not true.'

'Oh, trust me,' George smirked, 'it's true. Father was a soldier in both Boer Wars. Highly decorated, very brave, very strong. A *real* man.'

## The Pastoral

'If such a thing exists,' George added.

'I spent my entire childhood listening to his tales of derring-do. He was like a mythical hero.'

'So?'

'So I was never like that. I grew up reading. I like to write stories and poetry. I like painting the fields outside our house. I catch butterflies. Hardly the pursuits of a heroic offspring.'

'You mean, he wanted you to be more like him?'

'I think he wanted me to just be a man.'

'And a pre-requisite for manhood is to kill a man with your bare hands? Rather tribal, isn't it?'

'No, I just think he considered writing poetry and painting flowers...' he searched for the appropriate word, '...feminine.'

George chuckled. 'God knows what he'd think of *me* then. So you're here to prove something to your father, are you?'

'And myself I suppose.'

'You've nothing to prove son,' said George warmly.

'When I was twelve all the children in my school used to pick on me. I couldn't play football, I couldn't catch a rugby ball and I couldn't run very fast. I couldn't do any of the things that the others could do. And what was worse was that I was top of the class. They hated that.'

'I see.'

'I used to sit in the playground away from all the others and either draw or write stories and poems.' George offered a sympathetic smile. 'Not that it particularly bothered me. I was happy with my own company. If they left me alone I was fine. But they rarely did. I often came home with bruises and grazes. I told my father I got them playing with the others.'

'And you never fought back?'

'I did once. Ross Eggleton. I was doing a little sketch in my book. It was a picture of my mother that I'd copied from a photograph. He took it off me and he drew glasses and a beard on it and ruined it. I lost it. I punched him in the head.'

137

'And what did he do?'

Humbert sighed. 'He knocked me cold.'

'Ah!' said George uneasily.

'They sent for my mother who worked at the mill up the road from the school. She picked me up and took me home. Later that night my father came home and clouted me for not defending myself. "Stand up for yourself you big bloody girl!" he'd say.'

'What about the whole *turn the other cheek* thing? Were you not raised a Christian?'

'Well, yes, but I rather think he chose to follow bits of the bible rather that the whole thing. Anyway he didn't read. He never read. He used to drink, but he never read.'

'I see.'

'Anyway I'm not sure that I turned the other cheek.'

'I don't follow.' George poured some more tea, offering another to Humbert, who politely gestured that he had had enough.

'Well, turning the other cheek is when you could use violence – knock somebody's block off, and you don't walk away. Apart from the once I never fought because I *couldn't* fight. I used to outwit them in an argument but when you are that young words don't really count for much. I'd win an argument but lose a fight.'

'So what made you think that the army was for you?'

'I don't know. I just knew that home wasn't for me - especially if *he* was there.'

George had run out of questions. The two of them sat there in the dug out as night drew nearer. Humbert looked at George for a while and then smiled admiringly before taking to his feet.

'Well, thank you for the drink, sir?'

George stood up too. 'Oh, that's okay. Are you sure you are alright?'

'Yes, thank you. I think I'm going to try to get a couple of hours sleep if that is ok?'

'Yes, I think that's a good idea.'

Humbert saluted weakly and left the dugout. George

returned to his chair, had another sip of tea and stopped to think about the things that Humbert had said. Then with a yawn and a sigh he continued to compose.

# CHAPTER TWELVE

The sticky summer heat was getting a little too much for Ralph. His clothes clung to him and with every movement his uniform seemed to tug at his skin, pulling it one way then another. As he sat outside the field hospital he mopped the sweat from his eyes and the back of his neck and hoped that the nearby English Channel might send one of its customary breezes a few miles south to offer some relief. He opened his water bottle and drank some warm water. Then he poured the remainder over his scalp and leaned forward, his head bowed wearily. He felt the water finding its way through the forest of brown hair and down to the tip of his well-defined nose. Drip, drip, drip. He closed his eyes and tried to imagine that he wasn't in France at all, but rather, in Sherringham with Adeline, playing duets, pottering around the garden, reading Whitman while listening to the goldfinches chirping in the fully-blossomed cherry trees. He concentrated hard and tried to recall the sound of her voice, the delicate tones and undulations, and the soft sighs of passion she would whisper when they made love. Ralph could hear them for a brief moment, but no sooner was she audible than the sound of the wretched bugler came back to haunt him. He tried to recall her sound once again but was interrupted by someone calling his name. He opened his eyes jadedly and there at the floor were a pair of muddy brown boots. It was Harry.

'Ralph?'

'Harry.'

'What are you up to, mate?' asked the genial Steggles.

'Nothing. Just resting.'

'Well, we can't have that. A chap like you might start to think if left to his own devices. Then it's all down hill from there. So, follow me.'

'Sorry.'

'Come on you posh boy, get up, I've got a surprise for you.'

'A surprise? What is it?' said Ralph, beginning to raise a smile.

'A surprise? Well it's when something unexpected happens!'

'You know what I mean, Harry.'

'Look, I'm not going to tell you or it won't be a surprise will it you daft sod.'

Ralph followed Harry in to the hospital, through the large arched wooden door at the front, into the large hall filled with recuperating soldiers, then on into the kitchen at the back. It was a modest kitchen with a simple stove and a small collection of silver pots and pans hanging above. There were metal cups piled high in the sink ready to be cleaned next to a cylinder of plates stacked unsteadily nearby.

'What's going on Harry?' asked Ralph whose increasing uncertainty had made his smile level out to a slightly worried-looking grin.

'Just wait here.'

'But, what for? What am I supposed to...' Harry was gone. '...do?'

Ralph wandered around the kitchen timidly, like a young boy on his first day in a new school. To distract himself he began to open all of the drawers in the kitchen to see what was there. The cutlery drawer was a picture of disorganisation. Knives, forks and spoons had been seemingly thrown into the draw. He closed it, opened the cupboard beneath the sink and a whole host of kitchen flotsam spilled out before him. He panicked and quickly returned the odds and sods in as messy a manner as he had found them. He then made the decision to keep his hands to himself. He leaned against the sink unit and waited patiently for Harry to return.

After a couple of minutes Steggles returned sporting a wicked smile.

'Right lads come on in.'

One by one a host of soldiers came into kitchen, each with their own war wounds, some visible, some not. Twenty-one men lined up in front of him and each saluted. Ralph was lost.

'Hello, everyone,' he said politely through his confusion. They all looked at Ralph as if expecting a speech. 'Um, forgive me, but I'm not sure what is happening here. Harry, can you help.'

'Well…' began Harry a little apprehensively, 'this is your choir.'

'I'm sorry?' said Ralph incredulously.

'These chaps are singers – well they're soldiers of course, but they can all sing. Well they can all hold a tune.'

'Oh?'

'Yes, they can all sing in tune to my harmonica – more or less.'

'More or less?'

'Well, no one is perfect.'

Ralph paused to gather his thoughts. He was taken aback by the situation. Now he was uncertain.

'Would you excuse us for one moment gentlemen?' He pulled Harry aside and took him into an adjoining pantry, complete with dozens of boxes of porridge, two dozen mouse traps and cob webs which hung like bunting from the ceiling. 'What are you doing, Harry?'

'It's okay, mate I'll help you.'

'I don't need help and I don't need this?'

'Why not?'

Ralph hesitated. 'Well… well I haven't got time for it. I'm… I'm too busy.'

'Oh, pull the other one.'

'It's true.'

'Hogwash! You have the evenings free and you've got a weekend off coming up.'

'Well yes but….'

'…But nothing; you'll only spend the time… thinking.'

'I can't. I've never conducted a choir before. Certainly not one with…' he reconsidered his tone and words, 'I don't even know if they can sing.'

'Teach them,' said Harry stubbornly.

A moment passed while Ralph looked for another excuse. 'I haven't got a piano.'

'There's a bloody great organ. Don't forget this is church.'

'I can hardly play a bloody great big organ while the patients are trying to rest, can I?'

Harry was stumped for a while, but smiled and clicked his fingers as a solution came his way.

'Well then we can use my harmonica.'

'You can't accompany a choir with a harmonica.'

'Why?'

'Because you can't.'

'But I can play the tunes, or at least give the soldiers their starting notes.'

'Bloody hell, Harry!'

'Look, I never said it would be perfect.'

'You can say that again.'

'But what is perfect here? We all have to make do.' Ralph sighed while Harry continued. 'You asked me what you could do? *This* is something you can do. It doesn't matter if this isn't performed at the Albert Hall, that's not what it's about? If you can take these men away from the war, even if only for the length of a couple of verses of *All*

*Things Bright and Beautiful*, then surely it's all worth it.'

'Oh, Harry! Ralph sighed. 'I can't do this.'

'Yes you can.'

Ralph shook his head and black cloud descended upon him. 'I just can't.'

'Look, you're a teacher aren't you? You have pupils, don't you?'

'It's not that simple, Harry.'

'Why not? What's difficult about it? You're the finest musician in all of Britain and you can't teach a bunch of amateurs? I don't understand.' Ralph was becoming more and more agitated as the relentless Harry continued to push. 'Just give me a reason. Is it because you can't be bothered? Is it because they are not professionals? Just give me one reason why you can't do this. Just one.'

Ralph erupted. 'Because it's all gone, for Christ's sake!' he shouted.

Harry was stunned into silence. He was motionless as he watched a tear well up in his friend's eye. Ralph brought himself back from the brink in as English a manner as he could. He inhaled deeply then let the air out slowly as he tried to calm himself.

'It's all gone.' He slid down the sink unit and sat lethargically on the floor.

'What's all gone?' asked Harry.

'The music.' Harry sat down beside Ralph. 'All the music; it's just... gone.'

'I don't understand.'

'Neither do I. All I know is that there is no music inside me, except for an annoying little bugle sound which won't go away.'

'You know you don't have to write anything for these chaps. Just guide them through *It's a Long Way to Tipperary*.'

'It doesn't matter. It's *all* gone. There's nothing there. I can hardly recall anything; my music or anyone else's. I can't remember the music I learned as a child, the tunes my mother used to sing. My head is full of the sound of shells exploding, gun fire, screaming men, screaming *boys* in the field and in the trenches. I can hear the planes flying overhead. But the only piece of music I can hear is that god-forsaken bugle.'

For once Harry was lost for words. Nothing could console Ralph. Harry watched a tear run down his friend's face. Ralph mopped his face with the palm of his hand.

'And do you know,' Ralph continued, 'I've been worried about my career. How selfish is that?'

'It's not selfish at all, mate.'

'Of course it is! Everyday thousands of men are being maimed or killed, their… their fucking limbs ripped off, their… their fucking intestines hanging out as they call for their mothers —we've seen it Harry. You and I, we've seen it. We've pulled the bodies of… of *children* out of the mud.' He banged the side of his head as if trying to dislodge something inside. 'And all I can think of is if I'll be able to pay for my second home.' His tone changed to that of piercing sarcasm. 'How will I manage to afford that lovely wine to go on top of the grand piano, next to the silver candelabra? How dare I!'

'Ralph, don't do this to yourself…'

'How *fucking* dare I.'

Ralph put his face in his hands covering the shame that only he could feel. He sobbed uncontrollably. Englishness, the stiff upper lip was forgotten. The tears seeped through the cracks between his fingers. The cries could be heard from the kitchen where the soldiers stood awkwardly. Harry became aware of mumbles and mutterings as they waited patiently. Ralph began to thump the side of his head with a tightly clenched fist. He began to hit his temple harder and harder, until Harry took hold of his wrists and restrained him. Then as the episode threatened to become more fraught with madness, Harry held Ralph tightly in his arms and comforted him as the cataracts of tears continued to flow. As he realised the magnitude of Ralph's sadness, he began to shed a tear of his own. The two friends held each other tightly as the sun, descending low over the French countryside, sent shafts of light streaming through the stained glass windows of the kitchen.

The following morning in a trench not far from the River Somme George stood perfectly still on the duckboards. He was eating a piece of bread which the troops had been lucky enough to receive from HQ. Ten feet in front of him, a chaffinch had landed softly on the trench wall and was singing the sweetest melody. The bird bobbed about playfully in a series of stop-start movements. George, little by little ripped off a few crumbs of his breakfast and, between the thumb and the index finger, flicked them toward the bird. The specks of white bread landed a few feet away from him and then with a bob of his tail and a flash of the vibrant hues of blue, white and pink, pecked at the food gratefully before flying off. George smiled. He was amazed that something so small and nugatory as a humble Chaffinch should bring such joy to him.

'Beautiful, aren't they?' said a voice from behind him.

George turned around to see Humbert leaning casually against the entrance to the dugout.

'Yes, they are.'

'Very common though.'

'Yes.'

'My favourite bird is the Dipper. I love to watch them scatting in and out of the stream by my home in Derbyshire. Really playful. I used to sketch them.'

'And what did your father think of that?' chuckled George.

'He hated it, of course.'

'We used to get lots of birdwatchers come to see them, they're quite rare. They'd trample around in their silly hats and binoculars. They were a rare old sight. They completely ignored the Robins and the Blue Tits and the Bullfinches. They were deemed too common, as if that should in someway lessen their beauty.'

'It's what we do.'

'What do you mean?' asked the boy.

'Well, when we become over familiar with something we start to become blind to its beauty, to the very things that drew it to us in the first place. We don't notice the daisy's in the fields because there are so many of them, but if you look at them you realise how beautiful they really are. Same with the Chaffinch. Look at the vibrant colours, they're amazing. But, if they were threatened with extinction, if they were reduced to a single male, how beautiful it would be.'

Humbert listened with his eyes as well as his ears, he fixed his gaze upon George as he spoke, as though he were concentrating on the words of a verbose orator. Music seemed to run through George's voice as Humbert fixated himself upon his superior.

'Yes, I suppose so, sir.' His deep blue eyes glazed as the two stared at each other.

'Right,' said George, who by this time was beginning to feel the pangs of awkwardness swelling within him, 'uniform inspection, I think.'

George wandered off down the narrow line of the trench, aware that Humbert was watching his every step.

The kitchen had been cleaned meticulously. It smelled clean and fresh. The huge, old oak table used to prepare the soldiers' daily infusion of vitamins and minerals, had been moved to one end of the room to allow twenty-one army personnel to form a line ready for their first session of as, what Harry had christened, *The Blighty Boys*. Ralph stood in the doorway and tried to remain inconspicuous but he was fooling nobody. The singers knew exactly who he was and, indeed, many of them were only there to simply be in the presence of the renowned Vaughan Williams.

As Harry warmed up the voices with some scales which were accompanied rather shakily on his harmonica, many of the faces could not avert their gazes from the doorway. Ralph, noticing this, became slightly perturbed and moved just outside. Harry, with his usual sparky character, managed to relax the troops with his quirky humour and soon laughter could be heard all around the hospital as those who could sing and those who were tone deaf became hilariously apparent.

'Alright,' said Harry jovially, 'where are our basses? Who can hit the low notes?'

The men, still a little shy, were slightly reticent to come forward at first. They looked at each other with awkward smiles.

'Right, I know. We'll go down the line and hear how low you guys can go.'

The soldiers looked at each other with light hearted panic before Harry duly went down the line of singers and listened to them singing descending scales which resulted in funny sounds and even funnier grimaces. Howls of laughter broke out. Soon the baritones and the tenors had been recognised and the singers were duly split into sections.

'Okay chaps,' said Harry, 'now we've established that most of you couldn't hold a tune with a bleeding bayonet to your head, let's get down to work.'

The sound of further uproars of laughter made Ralph, standing just outside the kitchen, smile and his curiosity got the better of him. He peeped his head around the door and saw the choir laughing hysterically.

'Okay, let's start of with something simple.'

'What?' interrupted Hawkins, a blond haired Londoner. 'Are we going to do the alphabet song?'

'All in good time,' replied Harry, 'we might have to work our way up to that one!'

The joyous laughter continued. The men were bent doubled in wild abandon which made Ralph, still spying in the doorway, laugh too.

'Okay, who knows *God Save the King*?' asked Harry sarcastically.

The group sang the national anthem in unison to the tonic supplied by Harry's harmonica. As the tuning strayed from one key to another, from out of tune to cacophonic, the laughter continued. For the next hour all those gathered in the kitchen were blissfully unaware that there was a war on. There was no thought of the vile things that they had seen or done, no reflections on the bloodshed, the horror, the fear or the death. The only thing that mattered was the music – no matter how awful it was.

Later that night, as Ralph and Harry prepared to sleep on the stretchers in the back of a blood-stained ambulance, they laughed about the evening's entertainment.

'You're good with them,' said Ralph. 'You're a natural. You can… perform, you can entertain. I couldn't do that.'

'Oh, what are you talking about, you daft sod?'

'No, I mean it. I can write, yes. That's the easy bit. But, the hard part… I leave that to others. I'm not a performer. But you! You really are a…'

'Show off?'

The two chuckled merrily as the night brought welcome relief in the form of a cool breeze. There was a pause from the two, the kind of comfortable suspension in conversation which is only capable between real friends. Ralph lay on his back and placed his hands behind his head. The sound of crickets lulled them into a peaceful state where contemplation could thrive and thoughts could come and go freely.

'What do you dream about, Harry?' asked Ralph.

'Why do you ask?'

'I don't know. Just curious I suppose. I mean, and I hope you won't take offence by this, you don't seem like one of life's thinkers.'

Harry raised a smile, 'Oh, thanks very much.'

'Oh you know what I mean.'

'Do I really?'

'Yes, and I really don't mean to give offence,' the tone softened, 'I respect you greatly and envy you.'

'Envy me? Whatever for?'

'Well, you seem to have an aptitude for not thinking?'

'What you mean is that *you* think too much.'

'Probably, yes.'

'I think about lots of things,' said Harry rolling on to his front, placing the pillow beneath his chin and sighing contentedly, 'but there's only so much that *my* brain will allow me to deal with at one time. I think about home, I think about my boy and I think about what will happen tomorrow. But I try not to think too much about things that are out of my hands. I can't go home, so there's no point thinking about how lovely it would be to see my son. I can't stop the war so there's no point over-thinking that subject. All I can do is what I *can* do. So dreams… that's all they are really. I suppose I have… ambitions, aims perhaps.'

'What's the difference?'

'I dunno.' He yawned and wiped his face. 'Dreams aren't real. They're unobtainable. Ambition is something you can make happen through hard work and time. I used to dream of being an actor. I even did a play at the local amateur dramatics group. I was shite. So I worked hard at my trade and became a little ambitious. That's enough for me. I'm happy for dreams to just be those things that happen during the night. Anyway what about you? What do you dream about?'

'I used to have beautiful dreams. I used to dream about Adeline, I used to dream about walking in the countryside in Norfolk, but lately my dreams have become…' Harry looked at him expectantly while he considered his words,' …disturbing.'

'In what way?'

'Some of them are strange.'

'Go on then.'

'Well, for example, there was a particular dream where I was in no-mans land and there are shells going off all around me and there's mud flying everywhere. I pull a soldier out of a shell hole, he's screaming in agony and I look down and see that his torso is ripped open, his organs and intestines writing like worms. I try to put him back together and so I just start throwing everything back into his torso. His screaming stops, I put my head on his bloody chest to listen for a heart beat. There's silence. Then I lift my head and I see that the body is mine. The face still, quiet… and dead.'

Harry took a while to take the dream in. 'And that was the strange dream. Fucking hell, mate, what was the disturbing one like?'

Ralph paused for a second. 'Well I'm not completely sure it's a dream.'

'I don't follow.'

'I sleep, then I wake up. Then I…'

'Yes, what?'

Ralph inhaled deeply. '…I see things. The other night I woke up and looked out of the ambulance and saw… Oh it doesn't matter.'

'No, go on, mate' Harry entreated.

'No, you'll think I'm going mad… *I* think I'm going mad!'

'Just tell me. I think you're a loony anyway.'

Ralph afforded Harry a faint smile then took a moment to consider what he was about to say. I saw a man in evening wear. He was musician. He stood outside the ambulance and played those two notes that I can't stop hearing. Then he walks past and that's it. He doesn't seem sad, he doesn't seem happy; he seems completely indifferent to everything. He plays, then he goes.'

'And I'm sure all the symbolism isn't lost on you.'

'Certainly not, old boy. Certainly not.' Ralph stood up and paced up and down the short aisle of the ambulance. And then there are the strange dreams.'

'All dreams are strange, Ralph.'

'You are in one.'

'Bloody hell, mate. That *is* strange. Nobody's ever dreamt about me before!'

Ralph raised a meagre smile. 'You and I are in the trenches. The line is full of dead bodies and you and I are having a cup of tea and you are smoking a cigarette. It is as if… as if we don't care. At the side of us there is a gramophone playing. I can't hear it, but it is playing because I see it spinning around. You and I pick up the discs and thrown them up in the air one at a time. As they fly up in the air the German's in the trenches opposite start shooting at them, as if shooting at clays. We are laughing and seemingly unconcerned about the bodies piled high around us.'

'D'you think that happens.' Asked Harry.

'What?'

'You know. You get used to the death and killing and you stop caring.'

'Maybe. When you've seen what we've seen, Harry, the *terrible* things we've seen, maybe the only way to function in this kind of place is to cut off all your emotions. At the moment every body that I bring in, every boy with a leg missing is someone's son or someone's husband. But maybe, if we are here too long they'll just seem like… like machines to be mended or scrapped.'

Harry stared out of the ambulance and into the night sky. He rubbed his tired eyes and felt the lethargy trudge though his veins, thick like syrup. He returned to his bed.

'Do you have nightmares, Harry?'

'No,' said Harry instantly, I'm too bloody tired for that!'

The two began to laugh softly but as the absurdity of Harry's words set in, they began to laugh louder and louder, and as the moon rose into the sultry night the two friends indulged themselves in a brief moment of pure happiness.

# CHAPTER THIRTEEN

The smell of tobacco was rich and drifted down the line of the trench. Humbert made his way through the men that cluttered the duckboards. The smell reminded him of home and for a moment he wished he was back in the drawing room enjoying the merits of his father's hard-earned affluence. However, the thought soon disappeared as he imagined his father storming into the room to chastise him once again. He felt uncomfortable with his father's masculinity which often morphed into full blown chauvinism, which on occasion had resulted in his mother receiving a split lip. He hated his father for that. The only time he had retaliated at his father was after he had raised a hand to his mother. His father had been drinking heavily and Humbert had heard the sounds of unreciprocated passion turning violent in the bedroom down the corridor. He burst into the bedroom and began slapping his father, who could do nothing but laugh at his pitiful attack.

Now as he weaved in and out of the men, all of whom were older and stronger than him, he began to feel conspicuous. He felt that every face was watching him and laughing. He was aware that the uniform which seemed to fit the firm bodies of the rest of the troops, seemed to hang off him like the baggy clothes that hung loose on a scarecrow in a cornfield. This was a world of masculine humour full of foul language, sexual innuendo and black, infantile comedy. Humbert understood this and in no way scorned it, but it simply wasn't his style. He made his way to the dugout and sat on a sandbag. He looked at his hands, untouched by the wear of time or toil they seemed perfectly clean. Private Boon came and sat down next to him.

'You alright our Humbert?' he asked in a strong homely Yorkshire accent.

'Yes, I'm okay, Boon. I'm just…' Humbert stopped for a second and thought. While one of the troops was showing an interest in him he felt he should take this opportunity to speak to him. The others had generally treated him with mocking contempt. It was rare that he could walk past one of the platoon without being subjected to invectives and insults. '…Well, no. Not really, Boon?'

'What's up?'

'D'you ever think you made a mistake? Enlisting, I mean.'

'Everyday.'

'Really?'

'Yes, but when it's all over I'll look back and be able to walk through town and everyone will want to know me. I'll be proud. It's set me up for life. Then, I'll look back and think it was the best thing I ever did. I don't want to be sitting in a nursing home when I'm older wondering if I ever really knew myself.'

'But what if… you know, if you don't get through it?'

'Well I won't care. I'll be passed worrying. But me Mum and Dad will be right proud.' 'Why do you ask anyway?'

'I'm not sure I belong here?'

'Fuckin' 'ell mate. No one *belongs* in a place like this. We're all here. That's it.'

'But you and the others seem so… brave.'

'Some would say we were stupid.'

'But you've fought. How do you silence that voice inside which tells you what you are doing is…' Humbert searched his brain for the right word, the most sensitive word.

'…suicide?' suggested Boon.

'Well, yes, I suppose so.'

'You can't. You just ignore it. You have to.' Humbert contemplated Boon's words and felt his face drop and his heart sink. 'Anyway it helps to have a good leader.'

'You mean Lieutenant Butterworth?'

'Yes. The chaps here would take a bullet for him, no question.'

'Why?'

'Because we know he'd take a bullet for us.'

'No question?'

'*No* question!' affirmed Boon.

At that moment George came down the line of the trench, stopping to ruffle the hair of Emerson and offer a smile and words of assurance.

'Hey up!' laughed Boon. 'Talk of the devil.'

'That's no way to refer to your superior,' joked George.

'No, Humbert and I were just talking about you, like.'

'All bad I imagine!'

The starry-eyed boy interjected, 'Quite the contrary.' His admiring eyes seemed to make George a little uncomfortable.

'You daft sods!' said George.

As George was about to enter the dugout Humbert called to him spontaneously and, seemingly, without purpose. 'Uhm, Sir?'

'Yes Humbert? What is it?'

Humbert paused for a while. 'Oh, it's nothing, Sir. I just wondered if you played chess at all.'

'Well, yes I play it. I wouldn't say I was particularly good at it. Why do you ask?'

'Well, I was wondering if you might like a game.'

'Yes, thank you Humbert. I'd like that. Tell you what,

why don't we have a game later this evening.'

Humbert smiled ecstatically. 'Thank you, Sir.'

George made his way into the dugout leaving the young soldier beaming with joy. Boon stared at Humbert and joked.

'You bloody creep!' he laughed.

'What?' asked the boy innocently.

The close harmonies weren't quite as close as they should be, but the friendships between the singers of the *Blighty Boys* and their amateur chorister was tight. Ralph sat just inside the doorway, resting his head on his knees and squinting at each and every dud note or misplaced harmony. The joy and laughter in the room was beyond reproach, while the music seemed beyond repair. On his harmonica, Harry would find the starting note for each section of the choir to help them on their way. The buzzing tones of untrained musicians straining to hold on to their notes would drive Ralph to despair, albeit with a smile.

'Right chaps, let's try Tipperary,' said Harry with verve. 'This time let's see if we can sound like a choir.'

The choir chuckled and Ralph raised a smile. Then, just as Harry was about to begin conducting the singers with a wooden spoon he turned and saw Ralph grinning in the doorway. He looked at Ralph firmly in the eye and offered a beguiling wink.

'Oh, I'm sorry everyone,' said Harry, 'but I um… I have to use the toilet, but fear not, my deputy will take over in the meantime. So without further ado please put your hands together for the one, the only, Mr. Ralph Vaughan Williams!'

The choir erupted into rapturous applause and whistles. Ralph on the other hand seemed terrified.

'Uh… well I um… no I can't….' said Ralph in vein over the celebratory din of the elated men. He turned to Harry who was laughing mischievously on his way out of the kitchen, and scorned him. 'Harry! You bastard!'

## The Pastoral

Ralph stood before the choir and listened as the euphoria faded to an expectant silence. The face of each and every singer was fixed firmly on him. Ralph began to sweat. His heart thumped and he could feel his pulse surge through his neck and into his ears. The bugle motif sounded, softly at first and then increased in intensity until it made him wince and almost lose his balance. He could think of absolutely nothing to say. As the silence extended the faces of the choir began to drop. They began to glance at each other awkwardly as the atmosphere in the kitchen became more and more tense. One soldier, a handsome young corporal named Peters stepped forward and approached Ralph.

'Are you alright, Sir?'

Ralph, disturbed from his trance, looked up at Peters and smiled, touched by his kindness.

'Yes, I'm fine, mister..?'

'Peters, sir.'

'Uhm… well, let's see…' said Ralph hesitantly. 'Let's try the Tipperary number, like Mr. Steggles suggested.'

Ralph counted them in and was just about to begin conducting when another soldier, a stout Glaswegian called MacPherson stepped up urgently and brought proceedings to an abrupt halt.

'Stop!' he yelled.

'What'? Ralph, along with the rest of the men, looked startled and confused.

'You can't do this, Mr. Vaughan Williams.'

'What?'

'Not like this, Sir.'

'What? What's wrong?'

MacPherson walked behind Ralph, reached into the cutlery draw and pulled out a wooden spoon. He turned and stood before Ralph and with as serious a face as he could offer, looked him squarely in the eye.

'Please, Mr. Vaughan Williams,' he offered the wooden spoon, 'you can't conduct without this.'

Ralph looked at the spoon and then at the stone faced

MacPherson and began to chuckle. MacPherson, in turn, raised a smile which crescendoed into a laugh. Within seconds wild laughter had returned to the kitchen. Harry poked his head around the door and watched with glee as the hilarity continued. He smiled to himself and, with a sigh of relief and satisfaction, left the choir to it.

When Harry returned later he saw the choir singing heartily, their faces fixed on Ralph's flailing arms and the passion in his eyes. Harry stood, once again in the kitchen doorway and watched the renaissance unfold. Ralph was animated, he was energised and it seemed as though each soldier was tethered to his heart, soul and mind, and all he had to do was pull the strings like a puppeteer. Harry noticed that his friend was, in essence, somewhere else. With each rising of his arms Ralph seemed to be lifting his choir (for it *was* his now) up to the heavens and beyond. The transformation had been miraculous, for both the choir and Ralph. Harry, who had been completely unaware of Ralph's national reputation, nor the extent to which he was lionised by the musical fraternity, could now understand what all the fuss was about. The singers were likewise revealed. Their voices soared, their harmonies as crisp as a winter frost, their rhythms metronomic and mechanical but fluid and responsive to each emotional nuance in the music. As the music came to a close with a heart pounding crescendo, leaving the kitchen silent in disbelief, Harry came into the kitchen and smiled at everyone, with a particularly proud stare for Ralph.

'I'll get my coat,' he smiled.

Later that evening Ralph and Harry sat themselves down on a tombstone outside the makeshift field hospital. They sang and laughed joyfully. Harry played *Greensleeves* on the harmonica and repeatedly played the wrong note to the constant hilarity of Ralph who was bent double laughing. As the hilarity abated to sporadic chuckles the two friends replayed the evening through conversation.

'Your face was a picture, mate,' Harry smiled.

'I could have killed you.'

'I know, I thought you were going to.' Ralph leant back on the tombstone. 'Thank you.'

'That's okay,' said Harry.

'No, I mean it. I wouldn't have done it unless you pushed me a little. I thought my life had gone. It sounds somewhat dramatic, I know – particularly when life really is being taken from thousands of men every day – but it's true. All I know is music. That's it. Okay, I can dress a wound and pull a body out of no man's land, but that's not going to last as a job is it?'

'Christ! I hope not.' Harry looked up at the sky penitently, 'I'm sorry!'

'But it's not just a job. It's more than that. It's vocational.'

'It's what you do.'

'Yes.' Ralph detected a hint of irony in Harry's voice. 'I know it sounds pretentious, a little high-and-mighty perhaps, but…'

'You don't have to justify yourself Ralph. You don't have to explain it. Not to me. Not anymore.' Harry leant back and lay beside his friend. 'You're a good man, Ralph. You have a good heart. A kind heart. When I first met you I realised that you were…'

'…Pompous?'

'Well, perhaps a little!' Ralph smiled. 'I didn't know who you were. You were just, there. I didn't know who you were from Adam. But, you know, that's not it. You're humble. You have all that talent, all that music but you treat me like… like I belong at your side.'

'Now who's being a daft sod?'

'I'm just a loud, uneducated cockney.'

'Education doesn't come into it,' said Ralph.

'I know. And the fact that I know it is thanks to you. But when I saw you conducting those guys – even if it was with a bloody wooden spoon,' they both smiled, 'I realised that… that's what you are. You are a musician. You are a creator. It's in your blood. There's a part of me which is a little jealous. I'd love to have that ability to move people the way you do. But I also see that it can sometimes eat you up – because you are always thinking. You have to. You are always looking at every little piece of life, of yourself, of the things you believe in and you don't always see the good stuff.'

'No, there are some truly awful things in my mind – especially here, in France. But you know, you need to have a slightly more positive view of yourself. I really admire your passion for music. There is no pretence, there's no show. It's all about the music. I think I had begun to lose sight of that. It was in danger of becoming… business for me. Five pound of harmony and a couple of ounces of melody.'

They both sighed contentedly and looked up at the night sky. As the crickets sounded and the distant din of shells peppering the mud in no-man's land, Harry turned to Ralph.

'Give us a kiss mate!' He rolled over on top of Ralph and began to kiss his face wildly to the light-hearted screams of protest from his friend. Hilarity ensued once again. 'Keep the noise down you old sod, you'll wake the dead.'

# CHAPTER FOURTEEN

The tea that morning was particularly foul at a time when a good cuppa seemed more of a necessity than a luxury. As persistent rain fell on the trench it added to the foot or so of water which had collected over the last week of heavy precipitation. Boon and Humbert, huddled together knee-deep in murky brown water, sipped their teas and simultaneously grimaced.

'What is that strange taste?' asked the boy.

'Petrol,' replied Boon.

'Petrol?'

'Yeah, when the petrol cans are empty they swill them out and then put t' drinking water in it. Of course you can never get rid of the taste. Not completely.'

'It's horrid!' moaned Humbert.

'I imagine you're used to a bit better than that, hey?'

Humbert was irked. 'What's that supposed to mean?'

'Oh, nothing but…'

'But what, exactly?'

'Well, you're rich, aren't you?'

'Comfortable. Not rich.'

'Okay, okay! But where I come from if you're comfortable, you're rich.'

Humbert began to fidget. He began to rub his collar line, roll his shoulders, stretch his neck by circling his head and scratched furiously. Boon took little notice.

'Have you seen the Lieutenant this morning?' asked Humbert.

'No, but I'm sure he's around here somewhere. He led a trench raid last night.'

Humbert looked horrified. 'Well, what if he didn't get back? What if he was killed?'

'It's alright, mate. He's fine. I heard him talking t' captain when he got back. He's okay, but we did lose Jayne and Walpole. Both shot to bits.'

'Oh no,' he seemed almost dismissive of the two departed soldiers, 'but Lieutenant Butterworth is definitely okay?'

'I said he was fine, didn't I?' Humbert sighed and swallowed hard. 'Anyway what is it with you two?'

'What d'you mean?'

'Well you're always together, aren't you? Every evening you're in that dugout with him. What are you up to in there?'

'What are you saying, Boon?'

'Well,' said boon shuffling uncomfortably from side to side as he struggled to find the right words, 'the rest of the boys are saying…'

'…Saying what?'

'Well, you know?' Humbert raised a questioning eyebrow. 'That you and him are… you know…'

Humbert felt uneasy. Any attempt he might make to repudiate the claim that he was emotionally involved with George needed to be tempered in the face of the truth.

'We just play chess. What's wrong with that?'

'Nothing, mate.' Boon raised his hands defensively to appease Humbert's consternation. 'I'm just telling you that's what people are saying.'

The boy continued to ruffle his collar and scratch his neck line. This time Boon took notice.

'What's the matter?' he asked.

## The Pastoral

'It's this damn coat,' he replied querulously. 'It's so bloody itchy. It feels like it's made from barbed wire, for God's sake.'

"Ere you are, let me have a look, you big girl's blouse.'

Boon stood behind Humbert, pushed his head forward roughly and ran his finger along his collar line. Then he took out his lighter and flicked it to a flame. The lad darted away quickly.

'What the bloody hell are you doing?'

'Come back 'ere, you daft sod. I'm trying to get a look at your collar. I can't see properly in this light. Now come back and hold steady, will you?'

Humbert resumed his position and Boon ran the naked flame along the collar.

'Oh, it's just lice.'

'What?' erupted Humbert.

'Yeah, it's fuckin' lice.'

Humbert, in fit of repulsion, began to take his jacket and shirt off. He rubbed furiously at his neck line, took of his helmet and ruffled his hair frantically.

'It's alright, you silly bugger,' said a chuckling and unsympathetic Boon. 'We'll sort it out. Just give me your shirt and I'll get a candle and run it along the seam – that's where they nest – and you'll be right as rain.'

'Have you had lice before?' asked Humbert as he continued his frenzied strip.

'Well, I think they had me actually.' Boon collected the boy's insect ridden clothes and headed of down the trench line, leaving his colleague half naked beneath the rain. 'Back in a mo.'

Before Humbert had lost sight of Boon as he headed along the trench the earth shook with two huge explosions. Humbert was thrown to the floor and, as earth and debris rained down upon him, he heard the deafening after-ring in his ears. The sound pierced through him, as though a hot needle was perforating his eardrum. Humbert was initially immovable; clinging to the sandbags which lined what was left of the trench. His pedicured nails gripped deep into the fabric like the talons of a hawk clinging on to its prey. Then his fear and terror reanimated his feet and he began to walk toward the smoking scene. Other soldiers began to barge past him to attend to the wounded. Humbert watched as the soldiers started to slow down and only when he arrived at the scene did he understand why they had halted their runs. A circle of soldiers were huddled in silence around a huge crater, at least four feet deep. In the side of the sodden wall of the filthy chasm Boon's torso and head were imbedded. From the torso, Boon's spine protruded like a flimsy fishbone, his eyes wide open. Other fragments of flesh and bone were scattered nearby but were beyond recognition.

Humbert screamed hysterically, his cries split through the air and cut through to the bones of those stood stone-like and in silence. He began to call out Boon's name before succumbing to the rising of vomit, creeping up through his throat. The boy turned away and threw up on the duckboards, which were now visible since the explosions had begun to drain away the stagnant water which he and Boon had waded in only moments earlier. He heaved and tasted the vileness from within before falling to his knees, the rain pounding down on his bare shoulders. He lowered his head and felt the rain gather into huge drops at the end of his nose, the perennial chimes of tinnitus began to slice though his head and his hands began to shake uncontrollably. He was deaf to everything around him. He couldn't hear the men shuffling around and gathering sacks to collect the fragments of bone and sinew from the scene, he couldn't hear the sound of the boys from the flying corps over head and he couldn't hear George calling his name. He only responded once George had placed his hand on his back. He responded slowly.

'Humbert, look at me!' George turned the child around and shook him. 'Humbert, look at me!'

The boy, the child, seemed unable to move with any fluidity, it seemed to take an eternity for his eyes to meet with George's, stopping and starting along their way. Kneeling on the ground, his hands fixed wrist-deep in the filthy mud, he turned around to see if the image of Boon sunk deep into the face of the shell hole was a dream. It was as real as the rain rolling down his face and soon he felt the next wave of sickness welling up within him.

'It's okay, Humbert. You're alright.' George picked him up and ordered Private Hendon to help take him to Captain Burnham's dugout. As Humbert was help down the line of the trench he heard nothing still. He was watched by the rest of the soldiers as George and Hendon carried him into the dank claustrophobic hole in the trench wall.

'Thank you, Hendon,' said the fraternal George. 'Now, I want you to go and do a head count for me. Check we're all accounted for.'

'We're all here, Lieutenant. It's just Boon that we lost.'

'Okay, but please just go and check for me.'

'Yes, Sir.' He made his way back out into the rain.

George guided Humbert to a small wooden chair at the Captain's table.

'Sit down for a minute, Humbert. I'll pour you a drink.' From beneath the Captain's bed George pulled out a bottle of scotch and poured it into a tin mug. 'In the circumstances I shouldn't think Captain Burnham would mind. Anyway he's at HQ for the rest of the day, so I won't tell if you don't.'

George's light-heartedness was misplaced on this occasion. Humbert made no acknowledgement that the drink had even been placed in front of him. His mind was missing. His soaking frame, weakened by fear and trauma, was present but George could see the initial stages of shell-shock. He knew it existed. Sometimes he felt as though *he* had suffered from it – nightmares and, on occasion, hallucinations. Now, as Humbert shook uncontrollably at the table, staring into nowhere, he saw the first signs of the psychological cancer which had initially been dismissed by the military establishment.

'Humbert.' George spoke quietly. 'Humbert!'

Still the boy stared beyond his superior. George reached out his hand and held Humbert's hand who retracted it quickly in fear.

'It's okay, Humbert. It's okay. It's me, George.'

The boy looked at him with startled eyes, wide-open and sunk deep within his pale face, still dripping with rain. George hastily pulled the blanket off Burnham's bed and placed it around the boy's shoulders.

'Here,' he said, 'this'll warm you up. Now, get this down you.'

George pushed the mug of scotch toward him and beckoned him to drink it. In jerking movements Humbert placed the cup to his lips and drank the booze. He coughed and spluttered.

'That's it, good lad.'

As the boy continued to shudder and shake George lit a gas lantern and brought it to the table. Nothing was spoken. For a minute or so George surveyed the boy's meagre body and realised just how thin he was. He seemed undernourished. His ribs protruded and were exposed like the rafters on the inside of a barn. His chest was as bare as the day he was born. George could just as easily imagined seeing him with a leather satchel and a lunch box, as he could a rifle and soldier's kit. George saw the child before him and shook his head.

'I should have sent you home. I should have reported you. You'd be at home now, where you belong. You say your father's an awful man.' He took another cup and poured himself a large scotch and consumed it all before slamming the cup down on the table. 'But I'm the one who kept you here. I let you stay. This is no place for boys. This is no place for *men*.' He stood up and made his way to the dugout doorway and looked into the rainy sky. 'This is no place at all.'

The noise died down. The din of shelling came to an end and the shuffling sounds of the soldiers walking up and down the trench ceased, leaving only the gentle pitter-

## The Pastoral

pattering of the raindrops flooding the duckboards once again. George stood in the doorway for four or five minutes until, finally, Humbert spoke.

'I w-w-was j-j-just talking to him,' George continued to survey the tumultuous skies outside. 'Boon. I w-w-was talking to him about the lice. He was k-kind.'

'Yes, I know.' Still no movement, 'He was a good man.'

'He made me laugh.'

'Yes.'

'He t-t-told me about his family. He had a wife. Her n-name was Sarah. She had l-long red hair and very f-fair skin. That's what he said. He had a d-d-daughter. Her name was Katie. She was four. He t told me that she was pretty and funny. She used to like it when he sang funny s-s-songs to her. He played the banjo. He was going to ask you if you would ask Captain Burnham to allow him to have it sent to him here. He said he was good on the b-b-banjo.'

'He told me that too.'

'Everyone was right about me; particularly you. I shouldn't have come. I'm n-not ready to see these things.'

George sighed. 'Nobody could ever be ready for this. Never. I'll be thirty soon. I should be settling down. I should be... grown up.' He turned his head slightly to talk to Humbert who continued to shiver like the reflection of the moon on a midnight lake. 'A few weeks before you arrived, Robertson – who also lied about his age – tried to inflict a Blighty wound on himself so he could go home – back to Ripley. He took off his helmet, pulled out the pin from his hand grenade, placed it under his helmet and held the hat against the trench wall. He thought the helmet would absorb most of the blow. It did. But it still blew his hand off. He didn't think that... well, he didn't think. And now I have these dreams where I'm at home in my house and I open a draw and find Robertson's hand, still animated and smoking. In another dream I'm at the piano. I lift the lid and there it is again, caked in blood and dirt, still moving, still smoking. I wake up and I am crying. It's fear. Pure, real fear. It's the kind of fear you feel when you are a child and you need the safety of your mother or your father. It's like... when I was seven and I was separated from my parents in London. I was so frightened. It's fear that's undiluted by reason. I haven't grown up. I don't think I ever will. War doesn't make men. All that rubbish about boys becoming men in battle, because they... because they stuck a bayonet in a German stomach or they shot him through the head – that's all it is - rubbish. I have seen the worst that man can do. I've seen men...'

George struggled to maintain composure. As he spoke something inside was breaking. He began to cry and his breathing became shallow. He reached out his hand for the support of the crooked frame which passed as a dugout opening.

'S-s-sir?' Humbert looked up to George. For once the confident cheery exterior was gone. The cloak of masculinity had fallen.

'...I've seen men calling out for their mothers with their last agonising breaths. I've seen blood and bones. And still I wake up crying like a toddler. I'm not a man. I'm just a scared-shitless... boy.'

George slumped down the frame of the dugout and collapsed to his knees. The tears flowed like the rain outside. He tried to retain his dignity in the company of Humbert. His cry was gentle and calm, rather than a hysterical outburst. The boy, still in his own shock, didn't know what to do or say. He watched his hero deconstruct right before his eyes.

'Are you okay?' George continued to weep. 'Lieutenant Butterworth, are y-y-you alright?

George was silent. Humbert rose unsteadily to his feet and as he did so the blanket fell from his shoulders. He took a number of very short and uncertain paces toward George, like a toddler taking his first bumbling steps. As he approached George he called his name again. He could feel his body still shaking but didn't know if it was the cold, the trauma or the emotions he was feeling as he inched closer to his hero. Humbert slowly extended his hand to touch George's shoulder then retracted it as uncertainty and confusion set in. However, his emotions compelled him to reach out again this time he made contact. His hand rested on George's shoulder. George's tears relented and he managed to subdue himself to a perfect stillness. The boy descended slowly behind him. He moved in close and placed his arms around George who became nervous and uncomfortable. George turned around to face Humbert.

'It's okay, S-s-sir,' he said softly.

George offered an awkward smile before lowering his head. Humbert gently raised George's chin until their eyes met once again. He repeated his shaking words of assurance and then leaned in and kissed George on the lips with all the tenderness he possessed. As he did so he felt a warmth surge through his body, a tingle in his fingers, an extra beat from his heart and the rising of his manhood in his sodden trousers. However, the moment was transitory. It seemed to last a lifetime yet it was over all too soon. George pulled away quickly.

'What are you doing?'

George stood up and looked down on the boy who, in turn, looked up at him with tired and dreaming eyes.

'What are you doing, Humbert?'

'I'm sorry. I j-just thought that…'

George cupped his mouth in his hands, moved to the other end of the dugout to the furthest point in the room away from the boy and rested his back against the wall. A silence ensued. The two stared at each other, both waiting for the other to speak first. George looked for words that would not send Humbert into complete neurosis, while the boy searched for words which would not make his hero think any less of him. Humbert finally relinquished his inhibitions, what else did he have to lose?

'I think I-I…' he stuttered and paused, 'I think I l-l-love you.'

'I know.' Another long protracted silence descended on

the dugout.

'It sounds silly, doesn't it?'

'No.'

'Well?' asked the boy cautiously.

'I'm sorry, Humbert.'

The rejection wounded the boy. He had seen the deaths of Boon and Hatfield and had had so far survived the carnage, but with George's refusal to reciprocate he felt his heart break. Even if he was to survive the war, he was sure he would not survive this. He looked at George and tried to retain his last shreds of dignity.

'I don't love you, Humbert. I can't love you. I just can't. I can't give you the love that you want. That's not my kind of love.'

Humbert stood up. He shivered as he felt the breeze from the dugout opening brush over his feeble, half-naked body.

'I d-didn't *know* that was my kind of love,' said Humbert, 'I've n-n-never… Not with a man. Not with a girl. It's never happened b-before. But you were there and… Maybe any kind of love would have done. I don't know. Do you think love can exist in a place like this?'

George said nothing. He rested his back against the wall but could find no response.

'Does l-love have any purpose in a place like this other than to remind you of the things that you've l-l-lost? Is it love that s-sends you out in front of your troops or is that j-just duty? Is it love which sends you out into no-man's land to pull a mere private out of the mud, or is that just your hum-manity? Perhaps it's love that compels you to f-f-fire a b-bullet through a stranger's skull… love of your c-country, love of your g-government. That's not m-*my* kind of love.'

Humbert took a final look at George, his deep blue eyes straining in the darkness of the dugout, turned around slowly and headed back out into the rain. George watched him disappear and then felt a single tear roll down his face.

## CHAPTER FIFTEEN

George listened intently as Burnham relayed his orders from HQ. The battle of the Somme was to enter its second phase. He stood to attention, stone-like and firm, but as the details emerged he began to shiver inside.

'Munster Alley,' said the Captain as he unfolded a map on the small table in the middle of the room, 'it's a communication trench. The mission is simple; capture the trench, cut off the communications.

'Do we know how many are in there, Sir?'

'Your guess is as good as mine, but I can't imagine they'll lie down and let you in through the front door.'

'No, Sir.'

'So the artillery will blow the doors open for us and then we will clear up. We are to simply… walk.'

'Walk?'

'Haig's view is that after the bombardment we should be able to walk to the Hun's trenches. We should preserve energy and walk. A creeping barrage.'

'Madness!' said George incredulously. 'They'll pick us off one by one.'

'We take the front line and then hold it. Then we wait for back up before moving on to the second and third lines.'

'Sir, we won't even make it to the front line. We won't make it out of the bloody trench.' George rubbed his head in disbelief. 'When do we move?'

'Seven days.'

'A week?'

'That's how long HQ feel it will take to adequately undermine the German defences. Then it's our turn. Any questions?'

'Yes, lots, but is there any point in asking?' said George sarcastically.

Burnham was unimpressed. 'Kindly change your tone Lieutenant.'

'Yes, Sir,' conceded George.

'Dismissed, Lieutenant.'

George placed his hat on and saluted before leaving.

That night George did not sleep at all. In his mind he played out various scenarios and considered what his response would be. He thought about how he might protect his men as well as himself. Then he considered how he might relay the battle plan to his men without succumbing to his own cynicism. He needed to try to convince the troops that they would be victorious even if he felt the cause was lost. At times like these he would speak with Ralph, who would invariably take a realistic and pragmatic view of things and break fears and concerns down into small chunks, making worries more manageable. Ralph had a way of bringing perspective to situations which would often seem overpowering. In the absence of his friend he decided to write.

*My Dearest Friend Ralph*

*Although I am unable to give details of our future plans, suffice to say that I fear this may be the last time I write. You used to talk about 'my God,' a great deal often in less than complimentary terms. You were right! He has forsaken me, he has forsaken so many of my men and he has forsaken this awful wasteland of blood and dirt. The war has taken my faith and my spirit is weak. When we spoke in 1914 before I left England I spoke about my resolve to see the Kaiser defeated – I was convinced that we would see the war through to the victorious end. Now, in my darkest moments, when I have been detailed to bury another boy, another son in an unmarked grave, I don't care if we win or lose. I just want to go home. I want to get back to the piano and do what I was put on this earth to do – write music.*

*I have, during my time in the trenches, continued to write music. I have been writing what will be my first symphony. I have notated themes, variations, rhythmic developments, formalised structures and now it is a case of putting the jigsaw together. At the risk of blowing my own bugle I feel that what I have written here will define this generation, it will set England alight and make her proud once more. You will be proud!*

*All I have is my hope. That is all I have to cling to. I wonder if hope will be enough. My dearest Ralph you are a good man – the best of men – and I hope that one day in this world or another we will sing together again.*

*Your friend, now and forever,*

*George*

Ralph listened to the nurses gossiping on the ward as the doctors, medics and ambulance personnel moved the beds to one end of the church. There was a fever of excitement on the ward. Hastily written programmes were handed out to the audience of nurses, doctors, surgeons, porters, cooks and visiting soldiers – one between two. Harry had organised the performance at extremely short notice against Ralph's advice. The choir was, in Ralph's opinion, nowhere near ready for a performance. Their articulation needed attention as did their tuning and the basses were particularly weak. Harry had dismissed out of hand such concerns as the worries of an old perfectionist. He argued that perfection from a group of amateurs was wholly unobtainable and that in some respect the music was of no real importance, what matters is that soldiers who had seen such profound ugliness could now attempt, at least, to sound profound beauty. Harry believed that in war, little moments of happiness are magnified and their beauty truly revealed. Yes, the choir may still have inadequacies of intonation, rhythmic discrepancies and rather shaky harmonies but it is better than the sound of rifle fire, shelling or the excruciating screams of agony from the moribund in no-man's land. In such times bad music is simply better than no music at all. Not that the music was bad; Ralph had nurtured the singers to the extent that some parts were sung with confidence. They struggled to take direction from their conductor but this was due to inexperience rather than ineptitude.

Word had spread around the hospital and soon the ward began to fill up. The concert was even visited by some visiting dignitaries, well-meaning Generals who offered words of comfort to soldiers in the hastily organised audience. Ralph watched them come in and take their seats on a bed near the front of the makeshift auditorium and offered a polite smile. However, the sight of their insincere pastoral care riled him. It's all very well, he thought, to offer support, encouragement, to tell the soldiers that they would be fine, that they would pull through, but those words were easily spared from their comfortable position thirty miles from the line.

The programme consisted of a number of tunes from the old to the new, familiar to the unknown. As well as the ubiquitous *Tipperary*, Ralph had also included an old favourite, *Linden Lea* along with various hymns which he felt obliged to include given the ecclesiastic surroundings. The inclusion of *Abide with Me* and *All Things Great and Beautiful* made Ralph uncomfortable. Within the choir there were a number of devout and pious Catholics and Protestants and finding the music which would be appropriate to each, or at least not offend the other, was often on Ralph's mind. Additionally, there were a few agnostics who felt uneasy singing anything sacred.

The Pastoral

However, all of the singers, all endowed with youth, kept their objections to themselves for the good of the music and the choir as a whole. Such mutual respect for differing views, ideologies, doctrines and dogmas impressed Ralph and he wondered how quickly the war might be concluded to the satisfaction of all parties if it were run by the younger generation which the establishment on both sides seemed so intent on slaughtering.

Once the generous crowd had assembled and taken their seats Harry made his way to the front and stood in front of the choir which were stood, knees shaking and hearts racing, in a well-ordered line. Harry cleared his throat.

'Ladies and Gentlemen, welcome to the debut performance of the *Blighty Boys*. The choir have worked hard for the past few weeks to bring you the wonderful programme of music you are about to hear. So, without further ado, please welcome the most respected composer in all of England, Mr. Ralph Vaughan Williams!'

Enthusiastic applause rang out through the ward as Ralph entered and took a bow. Then he turned around and faced his singers. From the wings stage right Harry played a note on the harmonica to establish the key before Ralph launched them into the first piece. As they sang the audience sat receptively and smiled to see the musical amateurs creating such pleasing music.

As he conducted Ralph felt endorphins rush throughout his body. Despite the choir's lack of professionalism, the verve and vigour moved him greatly and tingles ran up and down his spine and surged around the nape of his neck, the hairs standing to attention to each crescendo, each movement of the melody and every rich and crisp harmony. Energy gushed through every vein and artery enabling Ralph to throw his arms, his facial expression and, indeed, his entire body into conducting the soldier's. The tiresome bugle tune was silenced and for the first time in nearly two years he was exorcised of his demons. Within all of the violence, all the abhorrence, all

175

the blood, the bones, the sinew, the cries of grown men calling for 'Mum', the stench of acrid and putrid death all around – Ralph was seeing and hearing the sound of humanity at its best. He heard the sound of men creating rather than destroying. He saw men celebrating life rather that submitting to death. As the choir's voices soared he felt, as he had when he was young and idealistic like George, that music, art, beauty and creation would somehow pull through and that after the war it would be pivotal to both sides in rebuilding.

As he lifted the choir and the audience with the music Ralph realised that whatever had blocked his musicality over the last two years had been washed away. He knew. He didn't have to think about the music, he didn't have to follow the dots and scribbles on his manuscript paper, he didn't have any compulsion to follow the music at all. It just happened. He knew that he was little more than a vessel for the majesty of the music, like a lightning rod channeling the power of a fierce and wonderful storm. As the sound filled the hall, as the magic filled the air Ralph began to weep.

As the choir sang heartily the last few bars of music, as Ralph lowered his flailing arms for one final time, the audience held their breath. Then the final chord was struck and thunderous and rapturous applause rang through the church. Ralph held his pose for a moment then slowly turned around to see the audience on their feet. He saw the joy in the faces of men swathed in bandages, supported by wooden crutches, sat up in beds and rickety wheelchairs, orderlies, nurses, doctors, surgeons, stretcher bearers and ambulance drivers and was overwhelmed. He had received plaudits and even adoration from audiences in the past yet somehow this praise from a modest audience in a little church-come-hospital in the pleasant countryside of Northern France seemed all the more poignant. Not only had he banished his own demons throughout the performance, but now it was clear that this modest musical ensemble had somehow managed to assuage the pain, suffering, the nightmares of the whole audience even if such relief was ephemeral. The choir took a bow and basked in the audience's love and affection and their faces beamed with pride.

As the sound of applause continued Ralph took a second or so to take in the profundity of the moment. He looked around the church and through the crowd knowing that this moment would define and possibly shape his life from this moment to his last breath. As he gazed he saw a familiar face in the crowd, smiling, laughing and applauding wildly with the rest of the audience. He squinted his eyes to focus harder and then blinked hard. It was George.

Ralph made his way down the aisle to find his beloved friend but at every step was accosted kindly by members of the audience who wanted to shake his hand, pat him on the back and congratulate him. One teary-eyed Scot even pulled him close and embraced him. Ralph managed to wriggle free of the man politely and ran to the end of the hall. He looked left, right, forward and backward but could not see his friend. He ambled his way through the crowd in every direction searching for George, he tapped the shoulder of a soldier who, from behind, was a perfect copy of his friend, but as the soldier turned Ralph saw the kind smile of a stranger. The thirty-something soldier shook hands with Ralph and congratulated him on his efforts. Ralph did his best to hide his disappointment, he thanked the man for his kind comments and moved off into the crowd again. He continued his search for George, scanning the faces in the crowd and looking for anyone even closely resembling his friend. But George was gone. Ralph conceded. He stood in the middle of the church as the audience shuffled away and as the beds were put back *in situ*. Within five minutes or so the hall bore no signs of the musical festivities and once again the room was quiet and still. Ralph continued to stand. He thought of his friend and wondered if what he saw was a hallucination, a daydream of wish-fulfilment, or whether he had actually been there mingling at the back of the crowd. As the moments and memories passed Ralph came to the melancholic conclusion that George had not been there at all. If he had her would surely sought to talk to Ralph. He even entertained the idea that George was dead and that perhaps he had seen a ghost. This was out of character for Ralph who, a distant relation to Charles Darwin, was sceptical about things which could not be explained through empirical sciences. He knew that science had not revealed all of the answers but was wary of those who filled in the blanks with religious suppositions. Either way, once again, he felt he had lost his friend.

The trench was silent but for the occasional stray rifle fire. George's men sat in the mist of the still early morning together but alone with their own thoughts. Some were filled with sobering thoughts of death and mutilation while others tried to visualise their heroics and victory. Some tried to quell their fears by imagining their lovers, mothers, fathers, brothers, sisters and friends. Some tried to recall sights, smells and sound of home while others tried to think of nothing at all. George closed his eyes and allowed the sweeping melody of his own *On the Banks of Green Willow* to soothe his mind. Soon he was transported to an idyllic riverside by the river Wye near the border with Wales where he would spend his summer with his mother and father. He found himself lying on his back on sun-faded grass by the riverside, the light from the sun above weaving in and out of the overhanging trees. He could hear the sound of the stream rushing by and the rustle of the gentle summer winds in the branches above. The smell of the blossoms filled his body and could feel the warmth of the suns indeterminate rays soothing his closed and restful eyes. He heard the sound of children paddling in the water and smiled as the soft tones of their laughter came into his consciousness. Then he heard the sound of sweet birdsong, melodious and gentle, its loveliness catching the breeze and finding the ears of all around.

Then a distant explosion pulled George away from his reverie, but the sound of the birdsong continued. He looked up and saw his friendly visitor, the chaffinch, chirping away merrily on the duckboards below. He admired the birds bold colours, peaches, blues and oranges, and spent a moment soaking in its beauty and elegance in this most foul of places.

As he watched the bird bobbing about, Corporal Hughes looked at the bird with disdain. He snarled at the little finch as it sang its merry song and drew out his pistol. He took aim.

'What have you got to be so chirpy about, you little shit?'

He fired on the bird killing it stone dead. George leapt up and grabbed Hughes by the throat. In a swift movement, and to Hughes' surprise, the corporal was pinned to the trench wall by his throat. George removed his pistol from his holster and held it to Hughes' temple. Hughes was terrified.

'You bastard!' yelled George. 'You bastard!'

'I'm sorry sir, I was just....'

'What Hughes?' George squeezed the Corporal's throat. 'What was it Hughes?'

'It was just a bird Sir.' He gasped for breath as George's grip tightened around his neck. 'I didn't mean anything. I was just mucking about.'

'Just a bird, was it? Just a bird. Was that all it was?' George pulled back the hammer on his pistol and watched as a new wave of fear and panic set into Hughes' face. He felt powerful almost to the point of omnipotence. He could see the terror in the young soldier's eyes and it was all of his making. 'You are just a boy, Hughes. You are *just* a boy - a stupid little boy. Are you deserving of the same treatment?'

The other soldiers watched on anxiously, frozen at the sight of their steadfast and stoic Lieutenant losing all control. Millar stepped forward.

'Come on, Sir. He didn't mean anything by it. He was

just letting off some steam.'

George moved nose to nose with Hughes, the gun in his hand shaking and quivering. The corporal squinted his eyes waiting for the deafening shot to end everything.

'It was a life!' George un-cocked his pistol and slowly loosened his grip. Hughes spluttered and clattered to the ground in a heap. George's anger seeped away leaving only a tired and weary shadow of a man in its wake. 'It was a life, for Christ's sake.'

George dropped his gun to the floor, rested his back against the trench wall and slid down. He put his head in his hands and began to cry with what dignity he had left.

'It was alive. We're surrounded by the dead. They're lying out there in the mud. Even the trees have died. They're nothing more than charred skeletons. The grass – gone. Even some of the rats have forsaken this place. Within all of this grey came a little piece of colour and you destroyed it. It was a life for God's sake. There's not much of it around here. And you killed it. You killed it, Hughes.'

Ralph, Harry and a team of medics and ambulance men gathered around a fire in a field next to the church. Around the fire large tents had been erected to take in the wounded that could not be housed in the church itself. The fire sparked and spluttered. Burning embers popped and jumped out of the flames, one landed at Ralph's feet. He watched its light fade to a dull glow before finally dying in the mud. Not even fire was free from death in this place, he thought. Heading the medics, doctors, nurses, stretcher-bearers and ambulance men was a well-spoken tall middle-aged man, Captain Harper. He strolled around the fire with his hands behind his back. Occasionally he would stop to groom his bushy black moustache, a nervous mannerism rather than vanity, Ralph thought. Having called the personnel to attention he paced around the flames for a while before he actually spoke.

'Ladies and gentlemen, the offensive against Jerry will move into a new phase in the next few days. The battle will intensify greatly.' He stopped and paused. 'There *will* be a great many casualties. We've all seen a great deal throughout this god-awful mess, but all of our eyes will be tested to the limit in the next phase of attacks. The British, the ANZACs and the French will soon try to take the German lines around the River Somme.'

'Oh great!' said Harry under his breath.

'We will start to mobilise tomorrow morning and should be in position by late tomorrow evening. I would ask you all to check your resources; check you have a complete medical kit and ensure that everything is in order.' He took a deep breath and then cleared his throat, clearly considering the best way to impart unpleasant instructions. 'I would also like you all to ensure that things are in order for your families should… should proceedings take a turn for the worst. Ensure that you have said what needs to be said and do what needs to be done.'

Ralph and Harry looked at each other grimly. Even Harry struggled to raise a supportive smile.

'You will be in you usual teams, you have developed a good understanding among yourselves and I know you will all prove me, yourselves and, of course, your king proud.' Harper took another look around. He noticed the fear in the faces but offered them all a proud smile. 'Good luck to you all. God be with you, everyone. Dismissed.'

Slowly the medical personnel stood up and began to shuffle away. The fear among them all was palpable. Nurses embraced each other in tears, while the men walked away wondering how the hostilities had ever come to this. Harry and Ralph were the last to leave. They had watched the fire fade to a gentle glow in silence. What else was there to say? They headed for a patch of grass near the ambulances and took off his coat, placed it on the ground and removed a photograph of his boy from his trouser pocket. Then he laid down, faced the stars, placed the picture on his chest and sobbed.

'Harry? Are you okay?'

He lay perfectly still, but in the light from the moon

and the inconsistent illuminations from the fading fire nearby, Ralph watched a tear escape from the side of his eyes and into his hairline. Harry raised a half smile, a token but no more.

'Never better, mate,' he said, 'never fucking better!'

Ralph was lost for words once again. In the absence of conversation he decided that all he could do at this point was to be there for his friend. He sat down beside Harry as a breeze brushed past them, sending shivers up and down their bodies.

'I'm… scared, Ralph.'

'I know, my friend, I know. But we'll be okay. I've got a feeling.'

'You're not succumbing to all that spiritual mumbo jumbo, are you?'

Ralph smiled. 'No, but I can see why people look for something. I think I can understand why we feel the need to search for… something else. Nobody wants to believe that we risk ourselves in a place like this for nothing. If the worst does happen, I suppose we want to know that something better awaits us.'

'Maybe, but that's not what I meant. That's not what I'm scared of. I couldn't give to hoots about me. If I die, I die. It's as simple as that. Part of me is scared of surviving.'

'What on earth do you mean?'

'What I've seen, what we're *about* to see… I don't want to take all that shit with me through the rest of my life. I don't want to spend the rest of my life frightened of the night, scared of what dreams may come.' Ralph nodded in agreement. 'But I'm terrified of never seeing my boy again. I can't go through the next world - if there is one - without my boy.'

'But if there's no such thing as the next world, you won't know any different.'

Harry expelled a little chuckle. 'Crazy isn't it?'

'What?' asked Ralph.

'Well, most people worry that there might not be a heaven. I'm terrified that there is. Because without my boy...' Harry fought back a tear. 'Well, no matter how many angels there are, it would be hell.'

'I know, my friend.' Ralph placed his hand on Harry's shoulder. 'I know. I wish I knew what to say. I wish I knew how to say it. I flatter myself that I am a relatively articulate man, but...'

'Ralph?' interjected Harry.

'Yes?'

'Shut up, you old fart.'

Ralph chuckled. 'Get some sleep Harry.'

Ralph couldn't sleep. He wasn't alone. How could anyone sleep with the visions of what was to come behind their closed eyes? It seemed that the only thing to do was to not close one's eyes at all. His thoughts at that moment turned toward George. Where was he? What was he doing? How was he feeling? And, most crucially, was he alive? With the uncertainty of his own continuance in proceedings Ralph decided to put pen to paper. He left Harry sleeping, in dreams of his boy back home, and headed back toward the smouldering fire. He brought with him a gas lantern and set it down beside him.

*My Dearest George*

*I hope this letter finds you and finds you well. I am, it seems, a stubborn old man. I, like those of my generation who have prolonged this nightmare, have been infected with the worst kind of cynicism. I have seen what that cynicism can do to the minds and bodies of the young - of your generation. My hope is that illness has not run too deep in your blood, and the blood of those young men who know so much more than their elders. It is in the purity of the young that we must find and hold on to hope. I remember when I was young - it seems a long time ago now. I remember how my dreams gave me momentum. I remember how hope made each day exciting and filled it with promise. When I think of all the things I achieved, all the music I wrote - Thomas Tallis and, before the war, The Lark Ascending - I wonder if it would have sounded so new and fresh had it not been for the presence of hope and the absence of cynicism.*

*What was I thinking when I spoke so disparagingly about "your God." For all I know, he might be my God too. And, although I wonder where he was when the war started, I do wonder if he was there in the voices of the choir I conducted here at the hospital. If he was, he is a good God.*

*I told you such awful things before we parted in 1914. I told you them in the misguided belief that you might not fulfill your destiny as you saw it. I didn't want you to go, because I didn't want to lose you. I hope that when you return that you will be the same hopeful man I knew in better days and that you will not have become like the blind, cynical old man that now misses you so much.*

*So, what I'm trying to say, in a somewhat convoluted way is - you were right!*

*Your friend, as ever,*

*Ralph*

*P.S. I look forward to looking over the drafts of the symphony on your return.*

# CHAPTER SIXTEEN

'Oh, this came for you yesterday, Lieutenant,' said a stone-faced private. 'I meant to give it to you, I'm sorry.' He gave George a dirty envelope, it had seemingly been dropped in the mud at some point. George looked at it and saw that it was Ralph's handwriting, but this was not the time to read. There were distant rumbles in the air, like an approaching storm, a ferocious and violent storm of almost biblical magnitude. The fine rain in the oppressive air hung and swirled around. It crept into the clothes of George and his men as they lined up by wooden ladders which stood up at ten-yard intervals along the trench. George put the letter in the top pocket of his jacket.

It was quiet, but not silent. As George listened to each and every breath as it thundered in and out of his body, he also became aware of other sounds. The sound of young men offering final prayers, the sound of crying softly and the occasional cry of those screaming in panic. He heard the sound of pistols being loaded, the click of bayonets being fixed to shaking rifles and the noise of men vomiting along the line. The smell of vomit began to sift through the already acrid air, George heaved. He looked along the trench and saw soldiers kissing crucifixes and faded and worn pictures of loved ones. He saw men stood still - frozen with fear and terror, he saw men shaking uncontrollably - unable to keep their rifle's steady. He also saw men punching the sandbags of the trench - some hitting out in anger, others trying to psych themselves for battle. Each soldier had his own terror, his own fear, his own realisation of the most dreadful nightmare and many of them could be seen trying to blink the dream away, hoping to find themselves in a warm bed in Harrogate or wherever home was. George watched men looking up to the heavens with imploring eyes and wondered where God was now. He was there for him when he wrote some of his finest music, but music didn't seem to matter at all; not now. Where was God now? How did he let things get this foul? All his faith in the bible, the teachings, in Jesus and in God himself has merely led him to this filthy trench before a sodden killing field.

Captain Burnham lifted the whistle to his lips and watched the second hand creep ominously toward the number twelve, and in those last few moments George heard the sound of birdsong floating through the air. Within all of the fear and the terror, it seemed the most beautiful tune he had ever heard. It could rival any Beethoven string quartet, any Mozart symphony, even a Bach cantata. The simplicity brought a lump to George's throat. All the tuition he had undergone as a child, all that he had learned about orchestration, counterpoint and musical arranging, yet he had never, and might never, match the beauty of a passing bird over no-man's land. He wondered why everything couldn't be as simple as the melody. Why was everything so complicated?

As the second hand drew nearer George drew a deep breath. His last thoughts were of Ralph. Flashing images of laughter on the beach creating songs, walking through the streets of flint-stone houses in Norfolk collecting folk tunes and sitting side by side at the piano improvising and sharing the deepest friendship. Ralph was more than a friend, he was an elder brother, a father figure, a confidant and constant source of inspiration and support. How he wished he could see him once more.

The whistle blew.

Burnham stepped up on the first rung of the ladder but before he could reach the second his face exploded in a mass of blood and bone, covering all those waiting to take the same perilous steps. His body flopped to the floor, his face smoking from the residue of the German snipers bullet. Hughes, at the bottom of the ladder, screamed hysterically. George took him by the lapels and shook him. This made no difference, Hughes continued his madness until George slapped his face hard. Hughes averted his eyes and George sent him on his way over the top, following on behind. The rest of the platoon followed on. George ran ahead of Hughes and took his place at the front of the procession of soldiers. He led them slowly. The warbling whistles of bullets splitting the wind fused with staccato sounds of the German machine guns, which were already ripping the flesh and bones of soldiers ahead.

'Hold the line, boys,' screamed George through the precipitation of lead, shrapnel and scattering mud. 'Hold the line! Don't run!'

Hughes by this point had succumb to panic. Unwilling to wait behind the slow procession of sitting ducks he sprinted on ahead.

'Oh, sod this!' he shouted and began to sprint toward the German lines. His face was filled with madness and violence as, seemingly possessed, he stormed ahead of his superior screaming at the top of his voice. Then he fell; into silence, into nothing. George sprinted to him and saw his body face down in the mud. He rolled Hughes on to his back and called to him.

'Hughes!' he cried, Hughes!' Nothing. Hughes' face was still, his eyes staring into nothing, the pupils fixed 'You bloody fool! George dropped his body unceremoniously back into the mud. George put his head in his hands, then, in anger he thumped the floor with the butt of his rifle. A shell exploded ten yards away which reminded him that this was not the time or the place for grieving. The men behind him had stopped and a bottle-neck had developed. He had to keep them moving.

'Onwards men!'

As they continued their way through the rifle-fire George would intermittently look behind to check on his men and each time he did so he noticed that their numbers were diminishing. He continued to walk forward, fighting the compulsion to run and wondering with each step if it would be his last. Then, with a deafening roar, a shell landed nearby. It splintered the air with burning shrapnel. George was thrown to the ground and as he surfaced he looked around to find his bearings and saw Millar walking around in circles holding his neck. George moved closer to him and saw that a six-inch piece of shrapnel had punctured his throat. Blood sprayed out down his hands and into his uniform.

'Millar! Get down!' shouted George. 'I'm coming for you now.'

George made his way to the disoriented Millar, but before he could reach him a soft thudding sound was heard and the back of Millar's head opened up. He folded at once and collapsed to the floor. George dived down and hid behind the body. He took two deep breaths and once again stood up and continued the suicide march. In the confusion, the soldiers had become detached from each other and George surveyed the battlefield for signs of his men. He knew that they would not have gone too far and so made for a shell hole from which he could call for his men safe, from the spraying lead. He landed in the shell-hole which was knee-deep in water. He called out to his men.

'Humbert! Heywood! Thomas! Emerson! Gulley! Forrester! Bartlett! Wilson! Henderson!'

Through the mud they came eventually, splashing down into the watery pit, crying, shaking and hyperventilating.

'How many are we?' George asked. 'Where's Heywood?

Where's Bartlett?'

'Heywood didn't make it, Sir,' answered Thomas.

'Bartlett was with me, Lieutenant, but after that shell I lost him,' said Emerson. 'I don't know where he is now.'

With those words Bartlett, a slender clean-shaven Scot, emerged through the smoke and gun fire and landed in the shell-hole. The men hunkered up together and listened to George, with the exception of Wilson who was struggling to maintain his composure. He fought to catch his breath. The short, sharp, shallow breaths sent the diminutive balding into a full-scale asthma attack. Gulley, a kind unshaven Welshman, broke away from discussions to tend to him. He did what he could to calm him down. He encouraged Wilson to breathe with him, placed his arms around him and spoke softly into his ear. George continued to address the group who were now mostly waist deep in the muddy water.

'Right,' said George. 'We've all made it this far, that's good. Forrester, hand me your binoculars.'

The young but greying Forrester lifted the strap of his binoculars over his head and passed them to his superior. George wiped the filthy, brown water of the lenses and looked over the rim of the shell hole. He scanned the bleak horizon and looked in the direction of the German communication trench.

'Okay, gentlemen. I think the Gerry trench we're after is about a hundred yards over that way.' He pointed forward and to his left slightly. 'About ten o'clock. But before we get there we've got to cut through the wires, they're about forty yards from the target. We're going to need a lot of covering fire and distraction while we cut. And we'll have to cut quickly.'

'But we've only got rifles and pistols, Sir,' said Henderson. 'We can't compete with those machine guns.'

'Have you got any better ideas?' Henderson looked forlorn. 'We can't spend the rest of the war in this bloody hole. Anyway, we've got the Mills bombs. That might keep them occupied for a while. The artillery *should* have knocked out most of the firing capabilities.'

Humbert took the binoculars from George and looked over the brim of the mud hole. George was taken by surprise.

'Let me see,' he said adjusting the focus and squinting through the lenses. 'There's a couple of bodies near a mound of earth a couple of yards behind the wire. Look, Sir.'

George took the binoculars and once again looked out into no-man's land. 'I see them. What about them?'

'If we can get there quickly, Sir, we can pile those two bodies on top of that lump of earth and shield behind them while one of us cuts the wire. The others can fire from behind the bodies.'

George had no idea where or when Humbert had discovered his inner soldier but his plan made sense.

'Okay,' he agreed, 'and then the trench will be within throwing range too.'

'Yes, Sir.'

George looked Humbert in the eye and then nodded his head approvingly. 'Alright, let's try it. With each shell fire we'll make our way forward; use the debris and smoke as cover. This time we run.'

'But our orders are to walk,' said Humbert.

'If you want to walk, you walk. Does anyone have any questions?'

The men shook their heads in unison. George counted down from three and on one the men climbed out of the shell hole and back out into the battle. They ran as fast as they could but the water in their boots, the mud caked around their ankles and beneath their feet made every step a mammoth effort. A step seemed like three steps, a yard seemed like ten. Every step was pulled to the earth by the weight of physical and mental exhaustion. George led the way by example. As they headed for the rings of wire, shots rang out around them and the warbling whistles of passing lead stormed through no-man's land like a swarm of tiny insects, intent on murder. As he ran, George felt a thud on his upper arm but continued toward the target. Soon he felt the warmth and moistness of blood seeping through his clothes, but did his best to pay no heed to it. He turned around to check on the progress of the men behind and saw that they were all still following. After what seemed a lifetime the men made it to the mound of earth just before the wire. Gulley and Emerson pulled the nearby corpses to the mound then rolled the putrid bodies without ceremony on top. The soldiers then huddled up closely behind, their bellies and faces planted in the wet mud. George inspected the wound on his shoulder.

'Are you okay, Lieutenant?' asked Henderson.

'Yes.' George rubbed his shoulder, he saw the blood on his hand and then wiped it on the front of his sodden jacket.

'I've got the first aid kit here, I could have a quick look at it if you like.'

George barked at Henderson. 'I said I'm okay, for God's sake.'

Henderson moved away and hung his head. Humbert crawled to the front of the group.

'Give me the cutters,' he demanded.

'No, Humbert. Emerson will do it.' Emerson at the back of the group swallowed hard. 'You wait here.'

'I can run faster than Emerson.'

'I don't bloody care Humbert!' shouted George. 'You're under my command, so you do as I bloody-well tell you. That way you we might keep you alive.'

'But I'm telling you, I can…'

'Just do as you're fucking told!' screamed George as another shell exploded nearby. He turned to Emerson and handed him the cutters. 'Right, take these and cut hard and fast. We'll give you covering fire and we've got the Mills' so you should have enough time to get through.'

'Yes, Sir.' Emerson took the cutters in his hand. They were shaking incessantly.

'Are you sure you can do this for me?'

'Uh… Yes… I th-th-think so.'

'You can't think!' said George. 'You have to know!'

Emerson took in a huge breath and then exhaled. 'I can do it.'

'Right,' said George. 'On my mark.'

George gave the signal and Emerson threw himself over the bodies and into the lines of indiscriminate gun fire. George, Humbert, Forrester, Henderson and Gulley provided covering fire. The wheezing Wilson continued to try and control his breathing and occasionally hurled Mills bombs toward the enemy. Emerson ran as fast as he could but within a half a dozen steps a warbling bullet found its way firmly into his chest. From their view point they watched Emerson slow from a run to a staggering walk before watching him fall to his knees in the mud. He seemed to kneel there for an age. Then they watched the cutters fall from his hands. The moment seemed to stop. Time seemed to cease. The soldiers behind the mound were silent. Then George shouted.

'Emerson!'

The stillness continued. Emerson knelt motionless in no-man's land. Then from within the relative quiet a distant cracking sound was heard and the men watched as Emerson's head opened up with a shower of crimson. Finally, his body fell to the floor.

'Shit!' exclaimed George. He lowered himself back behind the mound of earth and human decay. 'Shit!'

With those words Humbert leapt over George, beyond the mound and out toward Emerson's body.

George was livid. 'Humbert! Come back!' As he shouted, a stray bullet hurtled past his ear and forced him to take cover again. From behind the mound George screamed at the boy.

'Humbert! What are you doing! Get back here, you bloody idiot!' The barrage of guns and shell-fire seemed to intensify. George covered his helmet as the rain of dirt and bullets showered down upon him. The sky became darker and louder by the second. Then, as a brief lull ensued, George took his hands away from his helmet and peeped over the mound. The boy had done it. He had cut through the wire and was sheltering behind the rusting metal crisscross stands which held up the wire.

'I'm through,' shouted Humbert, 'are you coming?'

George couldn't believe what he saw. Humbert had seemed to have lost all of his fear, a very dangerous thing to do here, thought George. Clearly his rejection of George had had a massive impact on his personality. Gone was the frightened child who could barely hold his weapon. He was still little more than a quivering waif but he seemed not to give any recognition to his feelings. He appeared numb. While he was glad that Humbert was helping the men achieve their objective, he believed that his recklessness was the action of a boy at the end of his emotional tether rather, than a brave hero.

George signaled to his men to make their way to Humbert. They erupted out from beyond the hill of mud and corpses and as fast as the mud around their boots would allow. They came within twenty yards of the communications trench and George sent a Mills bomb hurtling into the air and into the line of German soldiers and communications operatives. The explosion rocked the ground beneath their feet. George ordered his men to do the same. As they made their way forward they fumbled for their bombs and likewise sent the grenades on their way to the trench. As the smoke rose from the trench George and his men stormed the line.

George was first to jump into the trench. He landed at the feet of a German who was yelling and screaming in agony and the lower part of his arm missing and spewing blood. The mills bombs had clearly been effective. The German seemed almost to plead for death. George duly obliged him and fired a single shot to the head.

The Germans' response was swift. They came down the line of the bombed out trench with bayonets pointed perilously forward. They screamed and yelled as they ran but all had the same fear in their faces as the British boys. After two years of fighting from two hundred yards away they now saw the whites of the eyes of the Hun.

Henderson sent two bullets into the jugular of a small, squat German, He ran forward to complete the kill with a bayonet to the gut but George shouted to him to move on with the attack. He did so and sprinted over the blood-seeping body of the gurgling soldier to another oncoming attacker. He ended him too with a bullet to the head.

Humbert, Gulley, Forrester and Wilson fired and felled a handful of approaching Germans but soon it seemed that all the ammunition was spent, now hands, knives and bayonets had to be used. A German officer charged at George, his eyes red with madness, his bayonet raised. George quickly ducked away and the long blade found only the side of the trench wall. George forced the rifle from his hands and wrestled the officer to the ground. The two fell into a puddle of filthy water. The officer put his arms around George's neck and began to squeeze. George struggled to find the strength to escape and knew that his exhaustion would inhibit his attempts to break free. As his time and air seemed to be running out, he reached to his side and unsheathed his knife. With all his strength he skewered the officer's rib cage and twisted. As he twisted, he felt hot warm blood trickle through his fingers and felt the German's hold loosen. As soon as he could he broke free of the officer and forced him face down into the puddle to drown.

Humbert had pierced the torso of a low-ranker and was moving on further. For a split second George watched and wondered if he felt proud of the boy, who was overcoming his own fears or if he was heartbroken to see the boy losing his innocence in such a violent and brutal a manner. George knew that his own victims on the battlefield, those whose life he had taken would have their revenge in his dreams for the rest of his days; but Humbert was younger - he had more time to go through the nightmares, the flashbacks and the hallucinations that would follow.

George stopped for a moment and watched his men battling with their German assailants. Time stopped once again, sound and feeling disappeared again. For a second he saw children fighting in the school yard. He blinked the sight away and saw the boys that he had tended to for the last two years transformed from carpenters, bakers, farmhands, postal workers and even schoolboys into killing machines. Within a matter of minutes the boys had captured the trench. The communications dugout was in their hand but the cost of life was high. Henderson lay dead on his back with a gaping wound on his throat, his killer, in turn, laying dead on his body. A collection of enemy soldiers were scattered - mutilated, dead - along the trench. Gulley and Wilson took up positions at either end of the communications trench, securing it from advancing German reinforcements. All there was to do now was wait for the next wave of Tommies to relieve them.

For the next four hours the morning was punctuated with the sound of occasional shots as Gulley and Wilson held up their end of the line while George and Humbert leaned against the trench wall near a sign which read *Münster Gasse*. The fought to catch their breath but neither could manage a word. Around their feet lay the catastrophic destruction of human life which would indelibly mark their lives from now until their final heartbeat. The blood on their hands would never wash away, the smell of rat faeces, decaying flesh and gunpowder would mar every inhalation, the piercing ringing sounds left in their ears from the din of war would reverberate through their dreams to each waking moment. Nothing would be the same again. Loved ones would walk into a cosy living room and find them staring into the distance, beyond the colour of the flowery wallpapered walls into this monochrome moment of coldness.

'Are you okay George?' said Humbert.

George looked at the boy, ashen-white with but for a line of blood smeared on his cheek bone where he had wiped a tear away with bloody hands. George was taken aback. He became distant, almost appearing to look straight through Humbert.

'Sorry, I meant "Sir", are you okay, Sir?'

There was a long pause while George wondered who he was. Was he the George Butterworth - the promising British composer, who had the musical world at his feet? Was he Lieutenant Butterworth - leader of a collection of ordinary, but at the same time extraordinary boys and men? Was he simply, George - devoted friend to the great Ralph Vaughan Williams? Or, was he little more than a thug? A murderer? A man who had taken another's life, split a skull with a spinning bullet from a hundred yards away. Was he the man who had turned young men in to shadows of what they might have been? Rather than leading a group of heroes he wondered if he had created nothing more than a collection of ghosts, whose own experiences would haunt them forever.

'My name *is* George?' He smiled at Humbert.

Then there was a crack… and everything stopped.

# CHAPTER SEVENTEEN

'Ralph! Ralph!' screamed Harry. 'Get down!'

Ralph stood still motionless in no-man's land surveying all of the carnage. It seemed to stop his heart. It was though he'd fallen into a nightmare. There was no noise, just the sound of the blood rushing around his ears and his heart holding down an incessant pounding rhythm. Nothing could have prepared him for anything like this. The field was like a carpet in a child's untidy bedroom, scattered with toy soldiers and broken pieces all around. But this was real. Those lying on the ground were, themselves in pieces. The first wave of soldiers had made their way over no-man's land and, before the next wave would advance the medical corps personnel would peruse the mud picking up the pieces of flesh and bone and attending to the wounded. Before further thoughts could enter his head Harry grabbed him by the lapels and pulled him to the floor.

'For fuck's sake, stay down!'

As Ralph fell to the ground the deafening din of war returned and startled him into full consciousness. Harry was attending to a moustache soldier with a shrapnel wound to the thigh.

'Hold here!' ordered Harry as the rain began to fall.

'Yes.' Ralph put firm pressure on the gaping wound which seeped blood through the meagre bandages and on to his own hands while Harry gave the man water from his bottle and searched the man's pockets for his SFA (Small First Aid) kit. He found more bandages which Harry then applied tightly to the wound. The man was in silent agony. The burning pain had been replaced by numbness provided by rushing endorphins.

'What's your name, mate?' asked Harry.

'Peter.' His voice shook as he spoke.

'Right, me old mate,' he said placing his hand on the man's forehead, 'we're going to get you out of here, okay? Get the stretcher, Ralph.'

Ralph, crouching down, dragged the stretcher through the mud and helped Harry pull Peter onto it. The soldier yelled wildly as the movement triggered a surge of pain through his wounded leg. Harry took the back end of the stretcher knowing full well that he would be first in line for any gun fire from the Germans as they retreated back toward the British line. Relative safety was only a couple of hundred yards away, but Ralph felt he might never reach it. At the front of the stretcher he stumbled over the debris which littered the once-green field. Huge clumps of mud, discarded helmets, pistols, rifles, back-packs, bodies in various stages of decay and even limbs had to be carefully negotiated as they moved, as fast as they could, toward the recently-vacated British trenches. Harry and Ralph both felt searing pains storm through their muscles as the weight of the invalid soldier pulled them down into the earth. Their upper-arms, shoulders, forearms and thigh muscles began to seize up and lock in to almost unusable solid masses. Finally, they made it to the trench where they lowered him down quickly to the ambulance personnel who would transport him to the medical clearing station. Harry and Ralph also slumped down into the trench to catch their breath and massage their aching muscles, bones

The Pastoral

and joints.

They both took a sip of their water bottles before Harry looked at Ralph and nodded.

'Right, let's go again!'

Once again the headed out into no man's land and made their way forward. After a while they came upon a soldier who was lying on his back and taking short, shallow breaths. He seemed much older than most soldiers and Ralph wondered if he had lied about his age to serve. Harry stopped at his side and saw that the man's stomach had opened up and the grisly contents laid bare for all to see.

'Jesus Christ!' said Ralph

Ralph began to trawl through the contents of his MFA kit, but Harry placed his hand on Ralph's and looked at his friend in resignation. The man was past treatment. Once again Harry placed his hand on the soldiers head while Ralph looked on helplessly. Then he leant forward and kissed the man on his forehead.

'Mum!' the man whispered. 'Mum.'

Ralph watched as the fear and pain disappeared from the man's face, and with it, life itself. The eyes closed and the breathing stopped. Harry reached into the man's pocket and found a small note book with the man's identity in it. Harry looked inside briefly and then placed the book in his medical bag.

There was no time to consider the profundity of the moment, they had to continue forward - in any case profundities had become normality here. Harry made his way toward a tree stump, sticking out of the ground like an ugly tombstone. It was hollow and charred by fire, standing little more than three feet high. Crouching down behind it, with his arms wrapped around legs tucked tightly up to his chest, was a pale-faced, flaxen-haired soldier in his thirties. He was uninjured. There were no signs of blood, no abrasions, no bruises - not a mark. Harry moved toward him with Ralph lagging behind, and found the soldier shaking and shuddering from head to toe. Harry noticed that the flaxen corporal had something clutched tightly in his hand. His knuckles were white.

'Alright mate?' asked Harry.

The soldier was unresponsive and looked straight through Harry. His eyes were glazed, fixed on nothing and were completely undisturbed as Ralph waved his hand in front of his face.

'Are you hurt?' asked Harry. No response. 'What's your name, mate? What company are you with? Where's your CO?'

Still there was no reaction.

'What are you holding?' asked Ralph. 'What's in your hand?'

The soldier didn't move a muscle, they were rigid and taught, and once still he said nothing. Ralph moved forward carefully and slowly as he dared, He reached out his hand and as he did so the soldier began to shake more violently, his breathing quickened but still didn't make a sound.

'It's okay,' said Ralph as calmly as he could, 'I just want to see what you have in your hand. I'm not going to hurt you. I'm here to help.'

Ralph touched the man's hand so as to reassure him, but still he shook and quivered. He pulled the soldier's hand away from his chest. He fought to ply open the tightly grasped fist, digit by digit, and there inside were two severed fingers. As he released them the soldier began to weep uncontrollably. There was no voice behind the tears, just an empty whispering cry. Ralph looked at Harry and both knew that this was every bit as serious an injury as the physical wounds they had witnessed. The fingers which the soldier held in his hands would mark his mind indelibly for the rest of the man's life. Harry placed his arms around the man and held him close with all the love he could summon.

'It's alright, son,' said Harry as he pulled the man close. 'It's alright, son.'

With those words Harry closed his eyes and saw his

own son staring back at him with big blue eyes and a smile which warm the coldest of hearts. He removed the soldier's helmet and ran his fingers through his hair and felt his own boy's soft and silky locks. Harry felt pain and loneliness swell up within him and he held the soldier in his arms as though he were hugging his own dear son. As he held the soldier closely, Harry allowed a single tear to slide slowly down his cheek. Ralph watched on and, though time was of the essence, he didn't feel that he could break up the embrace just yet. Instead he allowed the moment to play itself out, beneath the wooden tombstone.

However, after a while Ralph began to feel uncomfortably exposed, despite crouching down behind the tree stump. He reached out to his friend, touching him softly on the shoulder as he embraced the soldier.

'Harry,' he said softly.

Harry turned his shoulder away from Ralph and held on to the soldier even tighter.

'We've got to get him out of here, Harry. We can't stay here.'

Finally, his friend started to relinquish his hold, but stopped short of letting him go completely, taking his hand and holding it tightly then kissing it softly. Ralph pulled Harry away.

'Come on Harry.'

Harry and Ralph pulled the soldier up from the mire, placing his arms over their shoulders, and leaving the hand-splitting stretcher behind. His legs were completely immobile and his weight pulled them down deeper in to the mud as, once again they headed back toward the home trench. The soldier continued his silence and gripped the severed fingers ever tightly. The sky around continued to thunder with lightening explosions and distant rumbles as Harry and Ralph dragged the man into the trench.

Exhausted, Ralph collapsed to the ground and laid with his head resting on the filthy, sodden duckboards as the soldier was taken away. His heart raced, as did his breathing, but Harry picked him up by the collar and dragged him back out into no-mans land. They searched the smokey horizon for casualties, following the same route they had taken, past the tree stump, picking up the stretcher along the way and further forward. Thirty yards or so past the stump they saw a young private lying on his side, his rifle at his side with the bayonet fixed. Mud was smeared over his face from ground where he fell. The mud matted his curly brown locks and had begun to dry. As Harry and Ralph approached they saw that the boy had a severe wound to his shin bone.

'It's alright, mate,' said Harry. 'We're here to get you. What's your name?'

'Humes. Private Humes.' He screamed in pain as Ralph inspected the wound.

'What company are you with?'

'What does it fucking matter what company I'm with?' He became agitated and his fear and pain could not be contained. 'Just get me out of here!'

Ralph looked at the leg. It was clearly broken.

'It looks like a compound fracture. Slap bang in the middle of the leg.'

'We need a splint,' said Harry catching his breath.

'There's nothing we can use though.'

Hums became more outraged. 'Come on you bastards, just get me out of here, for fuck's sake!'

'We could use the wood from the stretcher,' suggested Harry.

'How?'

'We could cut off one of the handles.'

'What with.'

'I don't know. He's got a knife,' said Harry nodding in Humes' direction.

'It'll take you ages to cut through that wood with that little blade.' Then Ralph had a thought. 'We could use the bayonet.'

'That's no sharper than the knife.'

No, not to cut it,' said Ralph, 'to use for a splint. Take

off the blade and fix it to his leg, then wrap the bandage around that.'

'I see,' said Harry. 'Good idea.'

Harry unlatched the blade from the end of Humes' rifle while Ralph removed a roll of bandage from his kit.

Right, Humes,' said Ralph, 'We need to put a splint on this. The quicker we do it, the quicker we get out of here. It's going to hurt.'

Ralph and Harry carried out the procedure as quickly as they could. Ralph held the splint in place while Harry secured it to Humes' shin who in turned screamed in agony. The shrill high-pitched din of his cry sent shivers down Ralph's spine. As they began to lift Humes, two cracks followed by warbling whistles could be heard, as two bullets split the mist as it flew inches past them. Then another crack could be heard followed by a light thud. The bullet had split Humes' skull, shattering on impact and covering both Ralph and Harry with blood. Harry and Ralph dived to the ground for cover.

'Fucking hell!' shouted Harry.

They covered their heads with their hands as the mud hailed down on them, before looking up to see the residue from the bulled rising from the shell of Humes' head. Ralph pounded the ground with his fist and anger surged through his body. Harry, likewise was overcome with emotion. He rose to his feet and, with fury in his eyes, hurled mud toward the German trenches. He snarled at them and hurled insults and invectives at them. Then, as his helplessness threatened to overcome him and with tears welling again in his eyes, he picked up the pistol from Humes' side and pointed it at the opposing trench. He pulled the trigger but the chamber was empty. He fired again and again but each time nothing happened and, in an act of futility, he hurled the gun at the Hun as return fire stormed toward him. Ralph jumped on him and pushed him down to the ground, holding him steady as he tried to break free. Soon Harry's fury abated, leaving him in the mud breathing heavily as Ralph's hold on him relented.

'I can't do this anymore, Ralph.' Harry removed his helmet and rolled on to his back. I can't do it anymore.'

'I know, Harry.'

'I've always done my best. I've done my best to be an optimist, I've done my best to keep laughing, keep smiling… but I'm not sure there is anymore trying in me.'

'We're almost done,' said Ralph knowing full well that the job was far from done. 'Just a little bit longer and then we go home.'

'Do you really believe that?'

'I have to, what else is there to believe in?'

Harry swallowed hard and then took in a deep breath. Ralph pulled his friend close and held him with all the love he had.

'Come on, old boy. Let's get going.'

In the distance, a hundred yards or so beyond the second line of barbed wire Ralph saw a flare rocket into the sky. They followed the call. As they marched through the grime toward the SOS they kept their heads down and saw that in places the ground was littered with body parts. Limbs, torsos and faces were trampled in the mud and paved a horrible way forward for them. Machine gun shells were scattered all around and where the mud had created small channels in the ground, filthy rainwater travelled through no-mans land carrying with it the blood of the British and German dead. In a brief moment of reflection Ralph considered the irony that the blood of the Hun and the British was flowing into each other. The same blood of youth and fear flowed on and would become one with the earth. As the blood collected into little pools with the rainwater, its vibrant red hue became diluted into a murky brown dirge.

Finally, Harry and Ralph came upon a huge shell hole with a deep pool of water at the bottom. They looked into the hole and saw a mass grave. Bodies of British and German soldiers lined the wall of the shell hole in an uneven line like incompetent brickwork. A blast of howitzer fire nearby forced the two friends unceremoniously into the hole. It was still and silent. The water at the bottom of the hole rippled with thousands of tiny indentations from the heavy and persistent rain. Occasionally, the surface shuddered with the explosions from nearby shells like little earth tremors. Along the brim of the hole rats scurried about preparing for the feast of flesh and bone which awaited them below. The hole and its occupants had clearly been their for some time as the decay on their bodies illustrated, as did the smell of ammonia from the rat faeces - they had clearly been dining for some time. Loose barbed wire snaked around the area, in, out, over and under the dead. If any place epitomised the waste, the squalor, the pain and filth of the war this was surely it.

'Jesus Christ,' said Harry.

Ralph looked around once more at the bodies. There was a German with a wound to the chest, one with a deep laceration to the neck and another with a two bullet holes in his face, one on either cheek - an entrance and an exit wound. Ralph, staring for a moment at the emaciated body surmised that he would have starved to death, that he had fallen wounded in the hole with no chance of rescue. There were also dead British soldiers. Harry noticed one without legs, maggots feasting on the open wounds and turned away to wretch.

Then Ralph saw a tiny movement on the other side of the hole. It was a small shuddering like the ripples on the murky water. Held up opposite them was a German soldier of no more that eighteen years of age. His sparkling blue eyes glistened in the dull smokey light of the hole and his soaking wet blonde hair, matted with mud fell, flat against his forehead. A trickle of blood from a head wound had rolled down the centre of his head and forked off into thinning tributaries down either side of his nose. His skin was pale, ashen - only given hues from patches of mud pasted on his temples and along his jaw line.

In the German boy's arms was a young British soldier, scarcely breathing but still alive. His breathing was shallow, his eyes only half open. The British boy, also a teenager lay with his back against the German's chest. The curly-haired Tommy had a gun shot wound to his chest and bruises to his eyes. With one arm wrapped around the chest of his enemy, the German soldier lifted his water bottle to the lips of the Tommy and allowed a few drops to trickle into his mouth and then lifted his enemy's chin to allow the water to be swallowed more easily. Then with such care, kindness and love the German boy began to caress the British soldier's forehead, like a father holding a son. He tasseled the boy's hair and, with the back of his hand soothed the Tommy. There was such reverence with which the German treated the British soldier, such warmth in his hold, such serenity in the way he applied his humanity and such humility that Ralph and Harry and could only watch on.

For far too long Ralph had seen the ugliness which his generation had thrust upon the battlefield. He had seen the unforgivable manner in which the generals had sent men and boys *walking* into such carnage to become little more than forgotten martyrs to a hopeless cause; there would be no winner in this war - only those who lost less. He saw how old men on both sides had prolonged the war and complicated it. Yet here in a hole in the ground, in the middle of the most foul place on earth, a simple Gerry could administer love, kindness and humanity to the very man he should be trying to kill. In a war where wisdom had seemed to disappear among clouds of artillery smoke and poisonous gas, it seemed the wisest thing to do - to care for another. The shaking German soldier had no care for lines on a map, no thought of ideology or political persuasion; he simply saw man suffering and came to his aid with what humanity the war had not stolen from him. Ralph had seen some of the most inhumane things that could be witnessed by any eyes and now he saw humanity begin to regenerate in the eyes of the enemy, and he felt his doubt and his cynicism about the human condition relinquish its hold on his heart, and somewhere inside, he

## The Pastoral

felt seeds of hope tingling. He looked at Harry, smiled and wept softly.

As the tears began to run down his face, leaving light streaks in his mud stained face, Ralph began to hear the bugle player's refrain. The motif, which had been silent of late returned and echoed a few times in his head, and Ralph feared that its relentless nagging might be back for good. However, after a couple of worrying repetitions, Ralph heard an extension to the melody. Its unfamiliarity surprised him. As he watched the kindness of the good German, he listened as a new melody unfolded in his mind.

But this melody, which was beginning to unfold in his heart as well as his head, was unlike any other that he had imagined. The pastoral sounds of the idyllic English countryside was no longer audible. The gentle tones of lambs frisking in the fields, larks dancing in flight above a summer meadow were now replaced by the sound of emptiness. Soon he heard the sound of a simple unadorned soprano calling like an angel. For a moment he entertained the notion that it was indeed a call from above, a lyrical benediction from another world, then his attention was drawn back to the music itself. The singing receded into the darkness of the moment and, as he watched the German caress the moribund body of the British soldier, a slow crescendo of basses and cello took the melody further. Then, following a moment of uncertainty from the violins and a pause for reflection the orchestra emerged to bring in a hopeful melody.

The sound of hope had been silent for Ralph for a long time. He'd heard something in the joyful musings of the idealists enlisting in the army in 1914, but this, he concluded, was the sound of, at worst misplaced patriotism and at worst, blind jingoism. That he could now see such tenderness in such barbarity, such care for life in the presence of such disregard for life, such love in the eyes of one so young, meant that finally he could hear the tones of hope once more.

# CHAPTER EIGHTEEN

The rain had relented. It had left its mark on the sludgy land but now the steady attrition of black clouds gave way to pockets of light blue sky. The setting sun did its best to poke through and shine its weary light upon the rows of dead lined up outside the clearing station. Those who had met their end with proud dignity on the battlefield of the Somme were now set down in grisly rows with little ceremony. Their faces often still expressing the agony with which they drew their last breaths, their gnarled limbs contorted by shell fire or mines, their bodies peppered with bullet holes and bayonet wounds.

Harry and Ralph had come to the end of a day to end all. They had witnessed the best and worst of humanity in the space of one shift and had escaped physically unscathed, although even now, both friends knew that their minds would be scarred for ever. They walked slowly, step by step, along the terraces of corpses and it was hard to believe that less than a day earlier they had been husbands, fathers, brothers, sons, uncles and lovers and soon they would be little more than a feast for worms. Ralph, now, more than ever, wanted to believe in something. As he looked at the faces of the dead at his feet he understood why people looked for God. They look because they need to have a reason. They need to know that somewhere beyond all of this iniquitousness, something benevolent must be awaiting to give the slaughter some kind of purpose.

'Apparently, we gained a hundred yards,' said Harry as he surveyed the bodies. 'I wonder, was it worth it?'

'Nothing could be worth this,' replied Ralph. 'Nothing. How could it possibly...'

Men, some wounded, weaved through the long lines of dead, looking for friends, sometimes they were found, sometimes not. Army chaplains offered prayers for the dead while medical staff, admitting defeat, pulled army blankets over silent faces. A couple of privates had the unenviable task of having to collect identity cards and even final letters to be posted to loved ones back home. For a moment Ralph imagined that knock at the door and wondered how one imparts such news. Then he remembered the informal line taken by the army in such cases - 'he died quickly, he felt nothing, he was highly regarded by everyone.' And, with that thought he felt further away from Adeline than he had ever felt before. He wanted to hold her, to tell her that everything would be alright, then he wanted to hear the same words returned. He wanted to smell her, the perfume, the lavender she used to bring in from the garden and place in his study, anything other than the putrid decomposition which was beginning to set in. He wanted to hear her soft tones, the long cello lines of vibrato which would grow with subtle intensity. In an adjoining field stretcher bearers, ambulance drivers, captains and anyone who had an ounce of strength left within them began the gruelling task of digging graves for the departed. Wooden crucifixes, fashioned from the wood from ammunition boxes, were placed on their chest ready for the next stage of the mass funerals, burial. Those toiling with shovels, pickaxes or even bare hands wore tiredness and sadness on their faces, and they wore them well. One could be forgiven for believing that they could quite easily lay down in the graves they had dug and sleep there forever. The fields were silent. Only the distant rumbles of artillery fire interrupted the stillness.

Ralph wandered the long lines and felt numb. Suddenly the few that he and Harry had managed to rescue from the mud seemed to pale into insignificance. Likewise Harry wandered helplessly looking at the names written on the crosses before coming to a sudden halt. The sudden stop seemed to leave him paralysed. His legs were completely immovable. He looked at the soldier before him and saw the clean, neat bullet wound to the head and recognised the name on the cross, though not the face. Slowly he turned to Ralph who was at the end of the same row of bodies and stared at him. Ralph made his way mournfully toward Harry and without words, without signal, without gesture - he knew.

Ralph came closer to Harry, his pace slowing and before he could focus his eyes on the awful truth, Harry spoke.

'Ralph,' he said with complete stillness, 'I'm sorry.'

Finally, Ralph glanced down slowly and then saw George's body at peace among the hundreds. For a second the world stopped. The sun, creeping through a gap in the clouds shone on George's face, accentuating his features. Ralph stared for a moment before his legs buckled beneath him and he collapsed to his knees. Harry reached out to touch his friend but Ralph scurried on hands and knees and picked up George's lifeless body and held it tight. He lifted his cold, limp arms and placed them around his neck. There were no tears, no screams of overwhelming grief, just a broken man holding a broken body. Then he laid his friend's body down carefully once more. He noticed that where the body had been laid George's shirt had come untucked. Ralph gently tucked the shirt into George's trousers and straightened his jacket; perhaps the last act of friendship, or maybe an act of paternal pride. As he placed his hand on George's chest he felt something in the jacket pocket. Ralph reached inside and found his own letter which he had sent before The Somme.

'Oh no!' said Ralph, hanging his head.

'What is it?' asked Harry softly.

'He never got to read it.'

Harry crouched down beside Ralph. 'Then read to him now.'

'What's the point? He's dead.'

'At least you will have said it.'

Ralph looked at Harry for a moment and then opened the envelope and read the letter. As he did so Ralph allowed his heart to open up and release his love for his friend. He permitted himself to lower the veil of his Englishness and let the tears fall from his eyes. As he read, Harry fought his own tears and held strong for his friend.

'I told you such awful things,' read Ralph, 'before we parted in 1914. I told you them in the misguided belief that you might not fulfill your destiny as you saw it. I didn't want you to go, because I didn't want to lose you. I hope that when you return that you will be the same hopeful man I knew in better days and that you will not have become like the blind, cynical old man that now misses you so much.' He sighed and then took a deep breath before declaring, 'So, what I'm trying to say, in a somewhat convoluted way is you were right!'

Ralph wiped away his tears, tried to regain some composure and then leaned forward slowly and kissed his friend on the head and then on the lips, before rising again.

'Goodbye, my friend.'

Ralph stood up once again and turned to Harry. Harry looked deep into his friend's eyes. They were brimming with sadness once again and red with fatigue, the smudges of muddy tear smears beneath the eyelids. But in the centre of the eyes, in the blackness of the pupils Harry noticed the sun, hurling shafts of light through the clouds, reflecting hopefully.

## August 26th 1958

Forty-two years on and once again the eyes were brimming with salt water. There were more wrinkles, more lines for the tears to negotiate as they trickled toward the jawline. The last moments of the Pastoral Symphony played out on the gramophone and Ralph looked at the picture of George in his hand. He turned it over and once again read the dedication - *Hope is all we have*. At that moment the door opened and Ursula stood in the door way, the light from the hallway shining behind her turning her into a beautiful silhouette. The shafts of light shining from behind her like moonbeams through the clouds at night.

'What is it my love?' she asked.

Ralph kept his eyes fixed firmly on the tatty photograph.

'His family were offered compensation, you know; less a shilling for the blanket that they buried him in. Bastards. With one hand they gave him the Military Cross and with the other they took a shilling for a lousy piece of cloth.'

Ursula moved out of the light like an angel and kneeled at Ralph's feet. She took the photo and looked at it.

'Is this George?'

Ralph nodded. 'He was my friend.' She held his hand and ran her fingers along the blue, raised veins in his hand. 'They named the trench after him, you know? The Butterworth Trench. He was shot by a sniper, straight through the head. They said it was quick, they said he would have felt nothing. They always said that.'

'Ralph.' She squeezed a little tighter and kissed his knuckles.

'Open the top draw of the cabinet.'

'Why?'

'Please!' said Ralph.

Ursula relinquished her grip and headed over to the cabinet by the door. She opened the drawer.

'There's a large brown envelope.' Ursula took it out of the draw and brought it back to Ralph. 'Open it.'

She reached inside and pulled out a number of musical sketches. 'What is it?'

'It was the future, but now it's the past.'

'I don't understand. This isn't your handwriting.'

'No, it's George's. These were his unpublished pieces, sketches. There's even a note book. It's got the sketches for his first Symphony. He never got to complete it. He could have been one of the greats.' Ralph paused. 'He *was* one of the greats, but nobody knew it.'

Ursula respectfully placed the paraphernalia back in the envelope and left it with Ralph.

'Weren't you ever tempted to finish them off? You know, like Sussmayer, finishing Mozart's requiem?'

'No, it was his music. It would have been like disturbing a tomb.'

'But nobody knew his music like you did.'

'No, but that's just the way it is. If it was finished he would have let people hear it.'

Ursula looked at Ralph and saw a frankness she had never seen. He was never one to open up like this, but could see that he had something to say.

'I spent years after the war trying to find my way back to the kind of hope that I had before George died. I tried to find my way back to the England that I wrote about before all of that... all of that destruction, all of that killing, all of that... waste. All of that *awful* waste. There were echoes. The fifth symphony, I was close with that. Even some of the film music had... echoes, but that's all they were. Don't misunderstand me, I am proud of my music, I love my music... but I do wonder what happened to that lark. It seemed to stopped singing after the war, like so many voices. Occasionally, I would hear from the *Blighty Boys*, they kept singing. A couple of them went back, one was killed at the Battle of Cambrai.'

Ralph placed the envelope on his lap and closed his eyes.

'I've hardly spoken about the war. I don't know why. Was I trying to forget? How could I forget? You *don't* forget things like that. I saw the best of men, and the worst. Those things don't just slip out of your mind. They've been there everyday and every night. Sometimes I wake up in the middle of the night and I see Harry standing at the end of the bed. He's smiling of course. Sometimes I see Humbert - he looks strong, but lost. Sometimes I see some of the men I saved, then I see the one's I lost. And then if I'm lucky I see George. But they never speak. They never say anything.' Ralph sighed deeply, his frail body wheezing as he inhaled. 'And now I'm so tired.'

Ursula looked deep into Ralph's watery eyes and rose to kiss him tenderly on the forehead.

'Come on, darling,' she said stroking his face, 'I'll make you a nice hot drink.'

Ursula made for the door and then stopped. She turned around in the heavenly light, smiled at Ralph and then left the room.

For a moment everything seemed to stop. Ralph listened to the silence of the room and, then in the stillness, he heard the refrain of the bugler's incompetent call, a sound that had echoed throughout his life since 1916, through good times and bad. Finally, the call faded away leaving Ralph to contemplate the quiet in his study.

Ralph closed his eyes and heard the echo of laughter. It was Harry.

'Hurry up, posh boy!' his voice was clear and bright. 'Come on you, old sod.'

Ralph opened his eyes but saw nothing but the door in front of him. He grew tired and with a heavy heart let out a gentle sigh. Then, as the air escaped from his mouth he heard George's voice. He'd longed to hear the voice. For forty-two years he did what he could to preserve George's voice in his head. He'd try to recall the sound of his friend singing, the sound of him laughing and the sound of him talking. Now, as his breaths grew shallower, he could hear it as beautiful as it had always been, as warm as ever.

'Time's up, Ralph,' said George. 'Time to go.'

Ralph let out one last sigh and opened his eyes to see George standing at the door.

'My dear friend!' he said through the softest of whispers.

'Well?' said George. 'Shall we?'

# Notes from the Author

This book is based around many of the facts that we do know. Rather than explain where fact and fiction begin and end I will merely state that my main intention when writing this novel was to hypothesise what might have occurred in the trenches and on the battlefield. To ensure that the story was authentic and respectful I took great influence from the stories of soldiers who shared their tales of The Great War. As such I am grateful to The Imperial War Museum for their insight and research opportunities. I am also indebted to the great work of Max Arthur whose excellent compilations of veteran's stories were also a great influence here. I was also influenced by the writings of Dr W H Rivers whose work on shell-shock was so crucial in identifying and legitimising the condition. I am also indebted to the Ralph Vaughan Williams Society for their excellent website which offered great information.

However, the most important thing for me was to treat the subject matter with the respect it deserves. I hope you feel I have achieved this. If in the process of reading this book you have been inspired to listen to the life-affirming music of Vaughan Williams, George Butterworth, Gustav Holst and other great British composers such as Gerald Finzi, Peter Warlock, Frank Bridge, Herbert Howells and others like them, no one will be happier than I.

Jon Lawrence. April 2014

# The Pastoral

Printed in Great Britain
by Amazon.co.uk, Ltd.,
Marston Gate.